SHAKESPEARE ON STAGE

AS YOU LIKE IT

HAMLET

JULIUS CAESAR

MACBETH

THE MERCHANT OF VENICE

A MIDSUMMER NIGHT'S DREAM

OTHELLO, THE MOOR OF VENICE

ROMEO AND JULIET

SHAKESPEARE FOR YOUNG PEOPLE

HAMLET

HENRY THE FIFTH

JULIUS CAESAR

MACBETH

A MIDSUMMER NIGHT'S DREAM

MUCH ADO ABOUT NOTHING

ROMEO AND JULIET

THE TAMING OF THE SHREW

THE TEMPEST

TWELFTH NIGHT

SHAKESPEARE ON STAGE

OTHELLO, THE MOOR OF VENICE

by
William Shakespeare

edited and illustrated by
Diane Davidson

SWAN BOOKS
A division of Learning Links Inc.
New Hyde Park, New York

Published by:

SWAN BOOKS
a division of
LEARNING LINKS INC.
2300 Marcus Avenue
New Hyde Park, NY 11042

Printed in the United States of America

Library of Congress Cataloging-in-Publication Data

Shakespeare, William, 1564-1616.
Othello, the Moor of Venice.

(Shakespeare on stage)
I. Davidson, Diane. II. Title. III. Series:
Shakespeare, William, 1564-1616. Shakespeare on
stage.
PR2878.08D38 1985 822.3'3 83-60730
ISBN 07675-0862-9

FOREWORD TO THE SERIES

Sometimes, in our desire to appreciate Shakespeare properly, we forget the obvious: that Shakespeare was not a schoolteacher, not a classical scholar, but a professional entertainer. He made his chief living in the theatre as an actor and producer. There is no evidence that he helped his fellow-actors Heminge and Condell preserve his works in print for readers. The plays were written to be heard and seen.

I prepared this adaption, cutting the text to suit an average audience, supplying the missing visual effects by descriptions, and adding explanatory notes in parentheses where necessary. The awkward ten syllable printed line has been discarded, as it does not appear in a living theatre production. Shakespeare's words, however, are not changed. But my efforts thus are incomplete. The plays should also be read aloud with a group of friends, for Shakespeare's words feel good inside the mouth, and his sounds are a delight to any ear. A great writer should be enjoyed with all the senses.

I described my approach to a friend.

"But you're not really changing Shakespeare," he said. "You're just directing his shows on paper."

"Yes" I answered, "that's my intent – to give his spoken words a natural background."

Perhaps Will himself would not be too displeased. To his Elizabethan age, a play was play, not work.

And so I think it sensible at first for people to read shortened versions of Shakespeare's plays, with immediate explanations, in order to become familiar with the stories and major scenes. Also the reader begins to tune his ears to Shakespeare's speech. Later, we gain even more enjoyment from the uncut manuscripts and from different interpretations, especially on the stage. But however we approach Shakespeare's great plays, we should take pleasure in them.

Diane Davidson

Fair Oaks, California
1985

OTHELLO, THE MOOR OF VENICE

CHARACTERS

The Main Characters

Othello, the Moor of Venice, a noble black general with a loving yet jealous nature
Desdemona, Othello's fair young bride, a lady of Venice
Iago, Othello's "ancient" or ensign, a minor officer with an evil disposition
Cassio, Othello's lieutenant, a handsome young gentleman from Florence

People of Venice

The Duke or Doge of Venice
Brabantio, Desdemona's angry father, a Senator
Roderigo, Iago's follower, a fashionable young fool in love with Desdemona
Emilia, Iago's pleasant wife
Senators, also called Signiors

People of the Isle of Cyprus

Montano, the young governor of Cyprus
Bianca, a pretty courtesan of Cyprus, in love with Cassio
Clown, a servant of Othello's
Several Gentlemen

Visitors to Cyprus from Venice

Lodovico, Desdemona's good cousin
Gratiano, Desdemona's old uncle

Others

Herald, Officers, Gentlemen, and Attendants

THE BACKGROUND OF THE PLAY

Othello, "the play of jealousy," is Shakespeare's simplest and most symbolic tragedy. It tells of the love of Othello, the great black general of Venice, for his lovely blonde bride, Desdemona. Their story ends when, tricked by the villain Iago, Othello murders his faithful wife in a fit of monumental passion. Yet the play is not merely a jealousy-and-revenge melodrama, for it has greater meanings underneath the surface.

Like Shakespeare's other works, this play expresses the theme that life is a conflict, not so much between Good and Evil as between Law and Chaos. The world, created from Chaos, still retains much of its chaotic nature; only civilization and self-control check this tendency to confusion.

For instance, in a city like Venice, known for its law courts, personal difficulties can be solved easily. In Act I, the anger caused by Othello and Desdemona's hasty elopement is smoothed over by the Venetian Senate. This minor problem and its sensible solution contrast with the major problem yet to come.

When the scene moves away from civilized Venice to half-barbaric Cyprus, at first all seems well. "If it were now to die, 'twere now to be most happy!" cries Othello with joy, embracing his radiant young bride. But soon the chaos of jealousy begins to emerge. There is no court inquiry to reveal Iago's plotting.

And far from the restraints of city life, Othello, the self-disciplined general of Act I, takes the law into his own hands, destroying his perfect love. With common sense, Shakespeare says man needs the corrective action of self-control or civil law in times of crisis.

Throughout this tragedy, more than in his other works, the main characters resemble symbols left over from earlier plays of the Middle Ages. Iago, completely evil, is the spirit of medieval Vice. The pure Desdemona seems the spirit of medieval Virtue. Othello, torn between believing one or the other, is the half-good, half-bad mixture in everyone, a great and flawed Everyman jarred out of control.

Yet the characters are not merely symbols; they are highly individual people too, with contradictory human natures. Obedient Desdemona neglects her household duties to hear Othello tell of far-off lands. Shy as she is, the maiden is the one who indirectly proposes marriage to the general. And Othello, the ideal warrior, is easily tricked into jealousy by his ignorance of Venetian social customs. Iago, also, is not only the spirit of Evil. He is the ambitious, clever man from the lower classes who will never be promoted simply because he is not a gentleman. The name "Honest" Iago, which people constantly call him, has a triple meaning: first, it shows that everyone trusts his rough nature; second, it shows irony, as Iago is the spirit of dishonesty ; and third, it labels him as hopelessly lower class, as only working men were called "Honest Peter," "Honest John," etc.

So matters grow serious when Honest Iago, the competent but coarse soldier, sees the inexperienced and gentlemanly Cassio promoted over his head to be Othello's chief lieutenant.

From the first moment of the play, Iago seizes any chance to make trouble. If he cannot win, neither shall anyone else. The darkness of the opening scene foreshadows the darkness of the tragedy to come.

ACT I

Scene 1

(At midnight, on a side street in Venice, two men emerge from the shadows, quarreling. One, dressed plainly as a low-ranking army officer, is Honest Iago, who has a coarse and energetic manner. His companion is Roderigo, a rich young fool who is exquisitely dressed in velvet. As Iago holds a torch high to inspect the doors of different fine houses, Roderigo pulls at his sleeve, whining that Iago never lets him know what is going on, although the rough soldier always borrows his money.)

Roderigo: Tush! Never tell me? I take it much unkindly that thou, Iago, who hast had my purse, shouldst know of this!

Iago: (Trying to get the silly fellow to listen.) 'Sblood, but you will not hear me!

Roderigo: (Referring to Iago's dislike for Othello.) Thou told'st me thou didst hold him in thy hate.

Iago: Despise me if I do not! *(He turns away from the houses to explain his grudge against his general, Othello the Moor, who has refused to promote him, although three important men pled Iago's case with their hats in their hands.)* Three great ones of the city, in personal suit to make me his lieutenant, "off-capped" to him. *(In anger, he boasts of his own ability.)* And, by the faith of man, I know my price. I am worth no worse a place!

(He imitates Othello's refusal.) Says he, "I have already chose my officer." *(Iago growls with envy at his successful rival, a gentleman with book-learning and no army experience.)* And what was he? Forsooth, a great arithmetician, one Michael Cassio, a Florentine—a fellow almost damned in a fair wife—that never set a squadron in the field nor the division of a battle knows! *(He despises the man of polite talk, not action.)* Mere "prattle without practice" is all his soldiership. But **he**, sir, had the election!

(Bitterly Iago recalls his combat experience with Othello, who now keeps him idle and becalmed.) And I, of whom his eyes had seen the proof at Rhodes, at Cyprus, and on other grounds Christian and heathen, must be 'calmed. *(Sneering at Cassio, the amateur officer.)* He, in good time, must his lieutenant be, and I—God bless the mark!—his Moorship's ancient. *(He spits at his low rank of "ancient" or ensign, as he again turns to look at the row of rich houses.)*

Roderigo: (With a flounce of his fashionable handkerchief in rage at the treatment his honest friend has received.) By Heaven, I rather would have been his hangman!

Iago: (Impatiently he shrugs, for any job has its disadvantages.) Why, there's no remedy. Tis the curse of service. *(He frowns at the new method of promotion by personal preference, rather than by seniority.)* Preferment goes by letter and affection, and not by old gradation, where each second stood heir to the first. *(Giving a rough grunt*

at Roderigo.) Now, sir, be judge yourself whether I love the Moor!

Roderigo: I would not follow him then.

Iago: *(Suddenly confidential, he puts his arm about his stupid friend's shoulders as he explains he works only for his own good.)* O sir, content you! I follow him to "serve my turn" upon him. We cannot all be masters, nor all masters cannot be truly followed.

(To the slow-witted Roderigo, who nods in agreement at every word, he explains the troubles of workers, like the faithful follower who ends his life without a job or pension.) You shall mark many a knave that wears out his time for naught, and when he's old, cashiered. Whip me such honest knaves!

(In contrast, some work for their own advantage, only pretending to be loyal.) Others there are who keep yet their hearts attending on themselves, and throwing out but "shows of service" on their lords, do well. These fellows have some soul, and such a one do I profess myself! In following him, I follow but myself. Not I for love and duty, but "seeming so," for my peculiar end. *(If ever he acts the way he really feels, he will put his heart on display for birds to eat.)* When my outward action doth demonstrate my heart, tis not long after but I will wear my heart upon my sleeve for daws to peck at. *(They chuckle together at Iago's cleverness.)* I am not what I am!

(Slapping Roderigo across the back, Iago moves away to examine another dark front door. Roderigo sits, looking at one particular house, which belongs to the rich father of the fair Desdemona, whom Roderigo has long desired. Biting his nails, he envies black Othello's luck in eloping with the maiden a few short hours ago.)

Roderigo: What a full fortune does the Thick-Lips own!

Iago: (With a plan to make Desdemona's father angry.) Call up her father. Rouse him! *(He wants Othello to suffer for his marriage.)* Poison his delight! Proclaim him in the streets!

Roderigo: (Pointing) Here is her father's house. I'll call aloud!

Iago: (Handing him the torch, he urges him to cry out as if the city is on fire.) Do, with like timorous accent and dire yell as when, by night and negligence, the fire is spied in populous cities!

Roderigo: (Taking a deep breath, he calls up to the carved balconies and dark windows of the house.) What ho, Brabantio! Signior Brabantio, ho!

Iago: (Lustily adding to the noise) Awake! What, ho, Brabantio! Thieves! Thieves! Thieves! Look to your house, your daughter, and your bags! Thieves! Thieves! *(He pounds on the door with both fists.)*

Brabantio: (An older man, he appears at an upper window in his linen nightshirt, half-asleep but alarmed.) What is the reason of this? What is the matter there?

Iago: (As he hides beneath the balcony, he shouts louder than ever.) Zounds, sir, you are robbed! For shame! Put on your gown! Your heart is burst. You have lost half your soul! *(As Brabantio tries to struggle into his velvet night-robe, Iago makes a gross gesture towards the city, where black Othello and blonde Desdemona are in their marriage bed.)* Even now, now, very now, an old black ram is "tupping" your white ewe! Arise, arise! Awake the snorting citizens with the bell, or else the Devil will make a grandsire of you!

Brabantio: (Horrified at the foul words.) What, have you lost your wits?

Roderigo: (Nervously polite) Most reverend Signior, do you know my voice?

Brabantio: Not I. What are you?

Roderigo: My name is Roderigo...

Brabantio: The worser welcome! *(He has told Roderigo many times that the love-sick fool cannot marry Desdemona.)* I have charged thee not to haunt about my doors. In honest plainness thou hast heard me say, "My daughter is not for thee!"

Roderigo: Sir, sir, sir...Patience, good sir!

Iago: (Interrupting impatiently) Zounds, sir, you are one of those that will not serve God, if the Devil bid you! *(He coarsely calls Othello an African stallion.)* Because we come to do you service and you think we are ruffians, you'll have your daughter "covered with a Barbary horse"!

Brabantio: (Peering again to see who is saying such filth.) What profane wretch art thou?

Iago: (In the dark, he makes an obscene gesture to match his words.) I am one, sir, that comes to tell you—your daughter and the Moor are now making "the beast with two backs"!

Brabantio: (A roar of rage) Thou art a villain!

Iago: (Roaring back, with a grin.) You are...a Senator!

Brabantio: (Ready to fight) This thou shalt answer! *(He sputters rage at the embarrassed young gentleman.)* I know thee, Roderigo!

Roderigo: Sir...I beseech you...Your daughter, if you have not given her leave, hath made a gross revolt. *(Pleading for Brabantio to search his house.)* Straight satisfy yourself if she be in her chamber, or your house!

Brabantio: (Now truly alarmed, he calls for candles.) Strike on the tinder, ho! Give me a taper! Call up all my people! Light, I say! Light! *(He leaves to seek his daughter.)*

Iago: (Satisfied with the uproar he has caused, he plans to depart, as he must not lose his position for betraying his general.) Farewell, for I must leave you. It seems not wholesome to my place to be produced against the Moor. *(He points towards the city inn where the newly-weds have gone.)* Lead to the Sagittary the raised search, and there will I be with him. So, farewell!

(Roderigo, alone, watches the front door open, and Brabantio, in tears, comes out, followed by his servants with torches and swords.)

Brabantio: It is too true an evil. Gone she is! Now, Roderigo . . . Where didst thou see her?...O unhappy girl! . . . With the Moor, say'st thou? . . . Are they married, think you?

Roderigo: Truly I think they are.

Brabantio: O Heaven, how got she out? . . . O treason of the blood! Call up my brother! *(He waves for the servants to go search for his lost child.)* Some one way, some another! *(To Roderigo)* Do you know where we may apprehend her and the Moor?

Roderigo: I think I can discover him.

Brabantio: Pray you, lead on! At every house I'll call . . . *(Shouting to his next-door neighbor, as he hammers on the door.)* Get weapons, ho! And raise some special officers of might! *(To the young man)* On, good Roderigo! *(Joined by neighbors and servants, Roderigo leads Brabantio to the inn where Othello and Desdemona lie.)*

Scene 2

(Outside the inn of the Sagittary, Iago describes old Brabantio's curses at the elopement to Othello, a handsome black prince of the desert, about forty years old. The Moor remains calm while his Honest Iago tells how he felt like murdering old Brabantio, though his conscience kept him from doing so.)

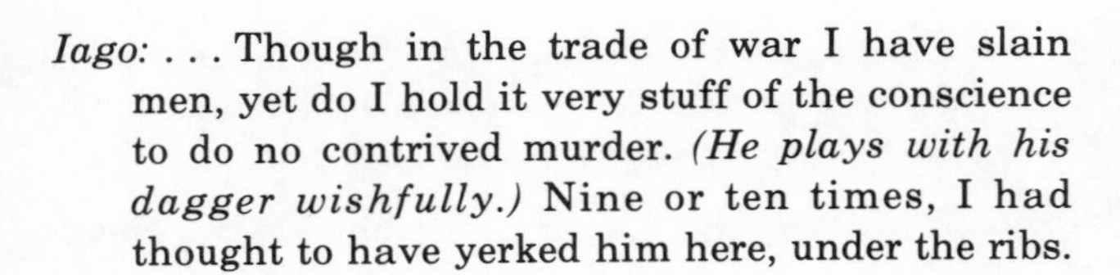

Iago: . . . Though in the trade of war I have slain men, yet do I hold it very stuff of the conscience to do no contrived murder. *(He plays with his dagger wishfully.)* Nine or ten times, I had thought to have yerked him here, under the ribs.

Othello: Tis better as it is. *(His quiet words show his self-confidence.)*

Iago: Nay, but he spoke such scurvy and provoking terms against your honor! *(Othello remains unimpressed, so Iago changes the subject.)* But I pray you, sir, are you fast married? *(As Othello nods gravely, Iago warns of Brabantio's many friends.)* Be assured of this, that the magnifico is much beloved!

Othello: Let him do his spite. *(He smiles slightly, knowing his good work for the Senate will outweigh any accusations.)* My services which I have done the Signiory shall out-tongue his complaints. *(He, too, is a nobleman.)* I fetch my life and being from men of royal siege. *(Except for love, he would not have given up his personal freedom.)* For know, Iago, but that I love the gentle Desdemona, I would not my un-housed free condition put into confine for the seas' worth!

(He glances down the dark street, where several men approach with torches.) But, look, what lights come yond? *(For a moment he does not recognize his new lieutenant, Cassio, among a group of officers of Venice.)*

Iago: (Still trying to alarm his general.) Those are the raised father and his friends! You were best go in.

Othello: (Standing still, sure of his high rank and great value.) Not I! I must be found. My parts, my title, and my perfect soul shall manifest me rightly. Is it they?

Iago: By Janus, I think . . . no!

Othello: (Recognizing the men) The servants of the Duke? And my lieutenant? *(He clasps hands with young Cassio, a handsome gentleman whom rough Iago regards with envy.)* The goodness of the night upon you, friends. What is the news?

Cassio: The Duke does greet you, General. And he requires your haste-post-haste appearance even on the instant!

Othello: (Immediately alert) What is the matter?

Cassio: (With a hint of an expected war.) Something from Cyprus, as I may divine. It is a business of some heat. You have been hotly called for!

Othello: Tis well I am found by you. I will but spend a word here in the house and go with you. *(He goes indoors to tell his bride he must report to the Duke and Senate. Meanwhile, Cassio asks Iago in a pleasantly superior manner why Othello is at the inn.)*

Cassio: Ancient, what makes he here?

Iago: He's married.

Cassio: (Startled) To who? *(Othello returns, carrying his sword.)*

Iago: Marry, to . . . *(Interrupting himself, he salutes his leader.)* Come, captain, will you go?

Othello: (Buckling on his sword, ready to leave.) Have with you.

Cassio: (As he points down the street, where more torches blaze.) Here comes another troop to seek for you. *(But the torches are held by Desdemona's father, Brabantio, with Roderigo, officers and neighbors, who stop a distance away.)*

Iago: It is Brabantio! *(In a whisper to Othello.)* General, be advised. He comes to bad intent!

Roderigo: (Nervously to the old father.) Signior, it is the Moor!

Brabantio: (Drawing his sword and urging his followers on.) Down with him, thief !

(Brabantio's group and Cassio's officers advance on each other with drawn swords. Iago, hiding a smile, chooses Roderigo for a mock opponent.)

Iago: You, Roderigo? Come, sir, I am for you! *(He lunges at Roderigo, who shrieks with fear and runs behind Brabantio.)*

Othello: (Moving between the two groups, he puts out his hand and speaks in a calm, deep voice.) Keep up your bright swords, for the dew will rust them. *(Over-awed by Othello's commanding presence, the fighters, one by one, put their swords away. The Moor continues to Brabantio, bowing with courtesy, as he says he will obey his old age rather than his sword.)* Good Signior, you shall more command with years than with your weapons.

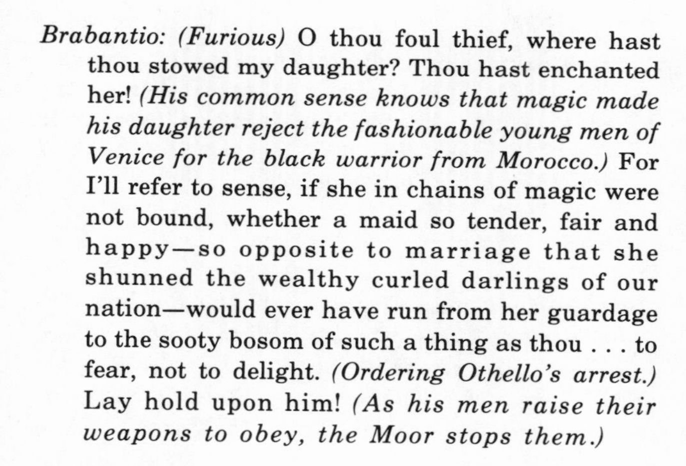

Brabantio: (Furious) O thou foul thief, where hast thou stowed my daughter? Thou hast enchanted her! *(His common sense knows that magic made his daughter reject the fashionable young men of Venice for the black warrior from Morocco.)* For I'll refer to sense, if she in chains of magic were not bound, whether a maid so tender, fair and happy—so opposite to marriage that she shunned the wealthy curled darlings of our nation—would ever have run from her guardage to the sooty bosom of such a thing as thou . . . to fear, not to delight. *(Ordering Othello's arrest.)* Lay hold upon him! *(As his men raise their weapons to obey, the Moor stops them.)*

Othello: Hold your hands! *(He knows when to fight without being told.)* Were it my cue to fight, I should have known it without a prompter. *(To Brabantio)* Whither will you that I go to answer this your charge?

Brabantio: To prison!

Othello: What if I do obey? *(He points to the Duke's officers, who came to fetch him.)* How may the Duke be therewith satisfied, whose messengers are here about my side upon some present business of the State to bring me to him?

Officer: (To Brabantio) Tis true, most worthy Signior. The Duke's in council, and your noble self, I am sure, is sent for.

Brabantio: (Alarmed, for he has not known the government is meeting.) How? The Duke in council? In this time of the night! *(Pointing to*

Othello, who must accompany them to the Senate.) Bring him away! Mine's not an idle cause. The Duke himself, or any of my brothers of the State, cannot but feel this wrong as 'twere their own! *(Together, they leave for the State council chamber in the Duke's palace.)*

Scene 3

(In the great council chamber, the Senators or Signiors sit at a council table with the Duke or Doge of Venice. Torchlight illuminates the worried faces of the men, who hold letters containing different reports about the invasion fleet of the Turks.)

First Senator: My letters say a hundred and seven galleys!

Duke: And mine a hundred forty!

Second Senator: And mine two hundred! Yet do they all confirm a Turkish fleet, and bearing up to Cyprus.

First Senator: (Seeing the new arrivals at the door.) Here comes Brabantio and the valiant Moor! *(Brabantio and Othello enter with Cassio, Iago, Roderigo, and the officers.)*

Duke: (Rising to greet his great general.) Valiant Othello, we must straight employ you against the enemy Ottoman! *(To Brabantio, with friendship)* Welcome, gentle Signior. We lacked your counsel and your help tonight!

Brabantio: So did I yours! *(In deep distress, he confesses nothing matters but his own tragedy.)* Good your Grace, pardon me. For my particular grief is of so flood-gate nature that it engluts and swallows other sorrows, and it is still itself!

Duke: Why, what's the matter?

Brabantio: My daughter! O, my daughter!

Duke and Senators: (In surprise) Dead?

Brabantio: Ay, to me. *(As they listen with sympathy, he explains that she has been bewitched from him.)* She is abused, stolen from me and corrupted by spells and medicines bought of mountebanks!

Duke: (Angrily promising that Brabantio himself can conduct the trial of such a magician.) Whoe'er he be that in this foul proceeding hath thus beguiled your daughter of herself and you of her, the bloody book of law you shall yourself read.

Brabantio: Humbly I thank your grace! *(He points to Othello.)* Here is the man . . . this Moor!

Duke and Senators: (Shocked) We are very sorry for it!

Duke: (To Othello) What in your own part can you say to this?

Brabantio: Nothing, but this is so!

Othello: (With a dignified bow to all.) Most potent, grave and reverend Signiors, my very noble and approved good masters—that I have taken away this old man's daughter, it is most true. True, I have married her! *(The listeners exchange looks of surprise, and Othello explains that marriage is*

Othello: Most potent, grave and reverend Signiors . . .

his only "crime.") The very head and front of my offending hath this extent, no more.

(He apologizes for his lack of fine manners.) Rude am I in my speech, and little blessed with the soft phrase of peace. *(From age seven until recently, he has lived only in army tents.)* For since these arms of mine had seven years' pith till now some nine moons wasted, they have used their dearest action in the tented field. *(All he knows is war.)* And little of this great world can I speak more than pertains to feats of broil and battle. And therefore little shall I grace my cause in speaking for myself.

(He hopes they will listen to his plain story, including any "magic" he has used.) Yet, by your gracious patience, I will a round, un-varnished tale deliver of my whole course of love: what drugs, what charms, what conjuration, and what mighty magic—for such proceeding I am charged withal—I won his daughter.

Brabantio: (Interrupting to describe Desdemona, a shy young girl.) A maiden never bold, of spirit so still and quiet that her motion blushed at herself. *(He cannot believe she was anything but frightened of the black Moor.)* And she—in spite of nature, of years, of country, credit, everything—to fall in love with what she feared to look on? *(Again he accuses Othello of using drugs on her.)* I therefore vouch again that, with some mixtures powerful o'er the blood, he wrought upon her!

Duke: (Stating that an accusation is not evidence.) To vouch this is no proof.

First Senator: But, Othello, speak! Did you poison this young maid's affections? Or came it by request, as soul to soul?

Othello: (To the Duke he appeals.) I do beseech you, send for the lady to the Sagittary and let her speak of me before her father. *(If Desdemona complains, they may remove him from office and put him to death.)* If you do find me foul in her report, the trust, the office I do hold of you, not only take away, but let your sentence even fall upon my life.

Duke: (To an officer) Fetch Desdemona hither!

Othello: (To Iago) Ancient, conduct them. You best know the place. *(Iago bows and leaves with two or three attendants.)* And till she come . . . *(Othello swears to tell the truth as if confessing sins in church.)* . . . as truly as to Heaven I do confess the vices of my blood, so justly to your grave ears I'll present how I did thrive in this fair lady's love, and she in mine.

Duke: Say it, Othello!

Othello: (Simply, he tells how, as Brabantio's guest, he often told stories of his military life.) Her father loved me, oft invited me, still questioned me the story of my life from year to year: the battles, sieges, fortunes that I have passed. I ran it through, even from my boyish days to the very moment that he bade me tell it.

(He lists some of the details of life as a soldier-of-fortune.) Wherein I spoke of most disastrous chances, of moving accidents by flood and field,

of hair-breath 'scapes in the imminent deadly breach, of being taken by the insolent foe and sold to slavery . . . *(He smiles to recall his freedom and his behavior throughout.)* . . . of my redemption thence and portance in my travel's history. *(He told Brabantio also of great caves, deserts and other isolated scenes.)* Wherein of antres vast and deserts idle, rough quarries, rocks and hills whose heads touch Heaven, it was my hint to speak. Such was the process.

(Strange creatures had he seen.) And of the cannibals that each other eat, the Anthropophagi. And men whose heads do grow beneath their shoulders! *(The Senate marvels aloud at his strange, romantic life.)*

(Sometimes Desdemona would slip away from housekeeping duties to listen to him.) This to hear would Desdemona seriously incline. But still the house affairs would draw her thence, which ever as she could with haste dispatch, she'd come again, and with a greedy ear devour up my discourse.

(Once when they were alone, he coaxed her to ask for his full story, which she had heard only in part.) Which I observing, took once a pliant hour, and found good means to draw from her a prayer of earnest heart that I would all my pilgrimage dilate, whereof by parcels she had something heard, but not intentively. *(She, listening, wept.)* I did consent, and often did beguile her of her tears when I did speak of some distressful stroke that my youth suffered.

(The Senators lean forward as they see how love began between the African warrior and the high-born maid of Venice.)

(Now Othello's strong face fills with wonder at Desdemona's behavior.) My story being done, she gave me for my pains . . . a world of sighs! She swore, in faith . . . 'twas strange, 'twas passing strange . . . 'twas pitiful . . . 'twas wondrous pitiful . . . she wished she had not heard it! Yet she wished that Heaven had made **her** such a man! *(She hinted that such a man could win her heart.)* She thanked me, and bade me—if I had a friend that loved her, I should but teach him how to tell my story, and that would woo her!

(The great general's voice, calm when speaking of dangers, grows shaken at the unexpected love he found.) Upon this hint I spake. She loved me for the dangers I had passed . . . and I loved her that she did pity them! *(To all he speaks the simple truth.)* This only is the witchcraft I have used.

(As Desdemona enters, he turns and holds out his arms to his lovely young wife.) Here comes the lady. Let her witness it! *(Before the entire court, she runs to him, and he embraces her fiercely.)*

(Clasped in each other's arms, they make a strange contrast, lovers from separate worlds. She is pale blonde, young, clad in a low-cut, elaborate silk gown of sophisticated Venice. He is black, mature, wearing the flowing white robes of the African desert.)

Duke: I think this tale would win my daughter too! *(To the outraged father, urging him to make the best of things.)* Good Brabantio, take up this mangled matter at the best.

Brabantio: (Stubbornly) I pray you, hear her speak! If she confess that she was half the wooer . . . *(To his daughter, sternly)* Come hither, gentle mistress. Do you perceive, in all this noble company, where most you owe obedience?

Desdemona: (Stepping forward towards her father, she speaks in a sweet low voice.) My noble father, I do perceive here a divided duty. To you I am bound for life and education. My life and education both do learn me how to respect you. You are the lord of duty. I am hitherto your daughter. *(Her father nods approval, but his face changes as she turns towards Othello.)*

But here's my husband! *(She will follow her own mother's example, leaving her family for her wedded lord.)* And so much duty as my mother showed to you, preferring you before her father, so much I challenge that I may profess due to the Moor my lord.

Brabantio: (Turning his back on her.) God be with you, I have done! *(To the Duke)* Please it, your Grace, on to the State affairs. *(To himself, bitterly, wishing he had not begotten her.)* I had rather to adopt a child than 'get it. *(To Othello)* Come hither, Moor!

(Othello advances, and Brabantio takes Desdemona's hand and lays it in the Moor's with disapproval.) I here do give thee that with all my heart

which, but thou hast already, with all my heart I would keep from thee. *(To the Duke, as he finishes.)* I have done, my lord.

(The love-sick Roderigo, watching, starts to cry. Iago motions him to be silent.)

Duke: (To Brabantio) Let me speak like yourself and lay a sentence which may help these lovers. *(He encourages the father to let bygones be bygones, or new problems will arise.)* To mourn a mischief that is past and gone is the next way to draw new mischief on.

Brabantio: Words are words. *(He does not think they cure anything.)* I never yet did hear that the bruised heart was pierced through the ear. *(Hoping to change the subject.)* I humbly beseech you, proceed to the affairs of State!

(All murmur agreement, and those closest to the newlyweds offer their congratulations. The Duke calls them to attention by standing and coughing, his letters in his hand. The Senate comes to order.)

Duke: The Turk with a most mighty preparation makes for Cyprus! *(To the general, who is familiar with the fortifications there.)* Othello, the fortitude of the place is best known to you. *(He hands him the letters and, with them, the command of the Venetian forces.)*

Othello: I do undertake this present war against the Ottomites! *(He pauses unexpectedly, wanting to find Desdemona proper living arrangements before he leaves.)* Most humbly, therefore, I crave fit disposition for my wife, with such accommodation as levels with her breeding.

Duke: If you please, be it at her father's...

Brabantio: (With a frown) I'll not have it so!

Othello: Nor I!

Desdemona: Nor I! *(She makes a deep curtsey to the ground, to ask a favor.)* Most gracious Duke, assist my simpleness!

Duke: What would you, Desdemona?

Desdemona: (She feels she has proved her love by running away with Othello.) That I did love the Moor to live with him, my downright violence and storm of fortunes may trumpet to the world! *(She loved the image of his mind.)* I saw Othello's visage in his mind, and to his honors and his valiant parts, did I my soul and fortunes consecrate. *(Now, if separated from him, she would lose all she tried to gain.)* So that, dear lords, if I be left behind, a moth of peace, and he go to the war, the rites for which I love him are bereft me. Let me go with him!

Othello: (Urging them to agree.) Let her will have a free way! *(He does not want her for pleasure but to ease her worries.)* Vouch with me, Heaven, I therefore beg it not to please the palate of my appetite, but to be free and bounteous to her mind. *(With her, he will not neglect his duty.)* And Heaven defend your good souls that you think I will your serious and great business scant when she is with me. No!

Duke: (Ready to agree with any quick decision.) Be it as you shall privately determine, either for her stay or going. The affair cries haste, and speed must answer it. *(Both Desdemona and Othello smile with joy.)*

First Senator: You must away tonight!

Othello: With all my heart! *(He salutes the Senate, and Desdemona curtsies in gratitude to them.)*

Duke: (To the Senators) At nine in the morning here we'll meet again. Othello, leave some officer behind, and he shall our commission bring to you, with such things else of quality and respect as doth import you.

Othello: (Introducing Iago as his messenger and Desdemona's escort.) So please your Grace, my ancient! *(Iago bows roughly.)* A man he is of honesty and trust. To his conveyance I assign my wife, with what else needful your good Grace shall think to be sent after me.

Duke: Let it be so! Good night to every one. *(As he leaves, he speaks to Brabantio, in praise of the Moor.)* And, noble Signior, your son-in-law is far more fair than black!

First Senator: (To Othello) Adieu, brave Moor. Use Desdemona well!

Brabantio: (With a final outburst of temper, he slings an awful warning at Othello.) Look to her, Moor, if thou hast eyes to see...She has deceived her father and may thee! *(He leaves with the other Senators.)*

(Othello and Desdemona stand frozen at her old father's warning. Iago's eyes gleam with quick interest. But Othello shakes off the curse and clasps his bride to his heart, sure that she will never betray him.)

Othello: My life upon her faith! *(To his ancient.)* Honest Iago, my Desdemona must I leave to thee. *(Iago bows, and Desdemona moves to give him her hand to kiss, which he does awkwardly, while Othello asks that Iago's wife be Desdemona's companion.)* I prithee, let thy wife attend on her, and bring them after in the best advantage. *(As Iago bows again, Othello takes Desdemona by the hand, for they have only a short time left to make arrangements.)* Come, Desdemona. I have but an hour of love, of worldly matters, and direction to spend with thee. We must obey the time! *(They leave, his arm about her protectively.)*

(Iago stares after them, deep in thought. But Roderigo creeps from a corner, broken-hearted that the fair Desdemona loves someone else. Finally he touches Iago on the shoulder.)

Roderigo: Iago?

Iago: (Startled from his thoughts, he answers absent-mindedly.) What say'st thou, noble heart?

Roderigo: (Sniffling) I will drown myself!

Iago: Why, thou silly gentleman?

Roderigo: (Looking after Desdemona) It is silliness to live, when to live is torment!

Iago: (In an explosion of coarse laughter.) O villainous! I have looked upon the world for four-times-seven years, and I never found man that knew how to love himself.

Roderigo: What should I do?

Iago: (Urging him to let his head rule his feelings.) We have Reason to cool our raging motions!

Roderigo: It cannot be!

Iago: (Passing off Roderigo's love as frustrated sex.) It is merely a lust of the blood and a permission of the will. Come, be a man! Drown thyself? Drown cats and blind puppies!

(As if kind, he puts his arm about the weakling's shoulders.) I have professed me thy friend, and I could never better stead thee than now. *(He motions towards the harbor and warships.)* Put money in thy purse. Follow thou the wars. *(Roderigo looks astonished that he too should go to Cyprus.)* I say, put money in thy purse!

(Iago gives hope for the future.) It cannot be that Desdemona should long continue her love to the Moor. Put money in thy purse! *(The Moor is too old, and she will soon turn to love young Roderigo.)* She must change for youth. When she is sated with his body, she will find the error of her choice. Therefore, put money in thy purse! Make all the money thou canst. Thou shalt enjoy her! *(Poor Roderigo gasps at the thought of Desdemona in his arms.)* Therefore, make money. A pox of drowning thyself!

Roderigo: (Running off) I'll go sell all my land!

Iago: (Giving a scornful laugh, he plans to trick the money from the dupe.) Thus do I ever make my fool my purse! *(But the thought of Othello stops his laughter.)* I hate the Moor! *(Gossip has reached him that Othello has seduced Iago's wife.)* And it is thought abroad that 'twixt my sheets has done my office. *(True or not, he will believe the rumor.)* I know not if it be true, but I, for mere suspicion in that kind, will do, as if for surety.

(Thinking how Othello likes him.) He holds me well. The better shall my purpose work on him. *(But he wants Cassio's position.)* Cassio's a proper man. Let me see now . . . to get his place . . . how? How? Let's see . . . .

(Inspiration strikes: he will make Othello believe that Cassio is having an affair with Desdemona, for Cassio looks the part.) After some time, to abuse Othello's ear that he is too familiar with his wife. He hath a person and a smooth dispose to be suspected . . . framed to make women false. *(Othello's unsophisticated soul will believe Iago, who will make him a donkey.)* The Moor is of a free and open nature that thinks men honest that but seem to be so, and will as tenderly be led by the nose as asses are!

(He laughs at his new-born plot.) I have it! It is engendered! Hell and night must bring this monstrous birth to the world's light! *(He leaves with high hopes for future mischief.)*

ACT II

Scene 1

(A violent storm rages over the island of Cyprus. On a cliff overlooking a seaport town, a gentleman stands watch, looking out to sea. On lower ground near the Quay are Montano, the young and earnest governor of Cyprus, and a Second Gentleman. They wait for news of the Turkish fleet and of Othello's Venetian ships, which are expected to join in battle soon. Neither navy is visible in the tossing seas. Montano, nervously playing with the gold chain-of-office about his neck, calls up to the First Gentleman, who is the lookout.)

Montano: What from the cape can you discern at sea?

First Gentleman: (Shouting above the storm as he peers into the thrashing waves.) Nothing at all! It is a high-wrought flood. I cannot descry a sail.

Montano: (Shaking his head, he doubts any ship could survive.) If that the Turkish fleet be not ensheltered, they are drowned. It is impossible to bear it out!

(For a moment, all that is heard is the wail of the wind, but over it comes a happy cheer from afar. A Third Gentleman enters, to announce that a Venetian ship has seen the Turkish fleet wrecked by the storm.)

Third Gentleman: News, lads! Our wars are done! *(Pointing out to sea.)* The desperate tempest hath so banged the Turks that their designment halts. A noble ship of Venice hath seen a grievous wreck on most part of their fleet!

Montano: (Overjoyed) How? Is this true?

Third Gentleman: (Pointing back towards the harbor, where he heard the news.) The ship is here put in. Michael Cassio, lieutenant to the warlike Moor Othello, is come on shore. The Moor himself's at sea, and is in full commission here for Cyprus!

Montano: (Happy to turn his authority over to so great a man.) I am glad on it. Tis a worthy governor! *(He takes the Second Gentleman by the arm.)* Let's to the seaside, ho! As well to see the vessel that's come in as throw out our eyes for brave Othello.

Third Gentleman: Come, let's do so! *(But their departure is interrupted by young Cassio himself, who arrives to greet the loyal men of Cyprus.)*

Cassio: Thanks, you the valiant of this warlike isle, that so approve the Moor! *(Frowning, he looks out where Othello's ship is still at the mercy of the raging storm.)* O, let the heavens give him defense against the elements, for I have lost him on a dangerous sea!

Montano: Is he well shipped?

Cassio: (Nodding) His bark is stoutly timbered, and his pilot of very expert and approved allowance. *(A cry comes from the harbor.)*

Voice: A sail, a sail, a sail!

Cassio: (With a prayer that the ship is Othello's.) My hopes do shape him for the governor! *(A cannon is fired from the harbor.)*

Second Gentleman: (Recognizing the salute to an ally.) They do discharge their shot of courtesy. Our friends at least.

Cassio: (To the Second Gentleman) I pray you, sir, go forth and give us truth who tis that is arrived.

Second Gentleman: I shall! *(He leaves at a run.)*

Montano: (To Cassio, eager for the latest news.) But, good lieutenant, is your general wived?

Cassio: Most fortunately! *(With a smile for Desdemona, who is superior to any report of her.)* He hath achieved a maid that paragons description and wild fame. *(The Second Gentleman returns from the harbor, out of breath.)* How now? Who has put in?

Second Gentleman: Tis one Iago, ancient to the general.

Cassio: He's had a most favorable and happy speed. *(But he gives credit to Desdemona, whose beauty has tamed the dangers of Nature.)* Tempests themselves, high seas, and howling winds, the guttered rocks and congregated sands, as having a sense of beauty, do omit their mortal natures, letting go safely by the divine Desdemona! *(He kisses his fingers in praise to her.)*

Montano: What is she? *(He smiles at Cassio's enthusiasm.)*

Cassio: She that I spake of. Our great "captain's captain," left in the conduct of the bold Iago.

(From the harbor come Desdemona, Iago, Roderigo, and Emilia, a pleasant-looking woman who is Iago's wife and Desdemona's lady-in-waiting. The women wear traveling cloaks with hoods. As Cassio sees them, he advances with courtly grace to kneel before Othello's beautiful wife.)

O, behold! The riches of the ship is come on shore! You men of Cyprus, let her have your knees! *(The others kneel also, as Cassio prays that blessings will surround Desdemona.)* Hail to thee, lady! And the grace of Heaven, before, behind thee, and on every hand, en-wheel thee round!

Desdemona: (Disregarding the flattery, she holds out her hand to Cassio with a serious question.) I thank you, valiant Cassio. What tidings can you tell me of my lord?

Cassio: He is not yet arrived. *(He rises.)* But he's well and will be shortly here.

Desdemona: O, but I fear! *(Her eyes fill with tears as she faces the wind.)* How lost you company?

Cassio: (With a gesture at the still-stormy sky.) The great contention of the sea and skies parted our fellowship. *(From the harbor comes another cry.)* But hark—a sail!

Voice: A sail, a sail! *(Another shot of courtesy follows.)*

Cassio: See for the news! *(The Second Gentleman dashes away again, and Cassio turns to greet Iago.)* Good ancient, you are welcome. *(He ignores the foolish Roderigo, but to Emilia he takes off his hat with a polite bow.)* Welcome, mistress! *(Iago frowns.)* Let it not gall your patience, good Iago, that I extend my manners. *(He excuses his courtliness by referring to his noble blood.)* Tis my breeding that gives me this bold show of courtesy! *(And he kisses Emilia on the mouth, in the best of high fashion.)*

Iago: (Snarling that if Emilia kissed Cassio as much as she nags Iago, Cassio would have plenty.) Sir, would she give you so much of her lips as of her tongue she oft bestows on me, you'd have enough!

(Emilia, overcome by the kiss, rolls her eyes and silently fans her mouth.)

Desdemona: Alas, she has no speech. *(All laugh.)*

Iago: In faith, too much!

Emilia: (Finding her voice) You have little cause to say so!

Iago: (Scornfully, he accuses his wife and all women of chattering everywhere.) Come on, come on! You are "pictures" out of doors, bells in your parlors, wildcats in your kitchens, saints in your injuries, devils being offended, players in your housewifery, and housewives in your beds!

Desdemona: (With disapproval) O, fie upon thee, slanderer!

Iago: Nay, it is true, or else I am a Turk. *(To him, women play at housework but make love a chore.)* You rise to play, and go to bed to work!

Desdemona: (Curiously, to the woman-hater.) What wouldst thou write of me, if thou shouldst praise me?

Iago: O gentle lady, do not put me to it, for I am nothing if not critical.

Desdemona: Come on. *(Nervously looking out to sea.)* There's one gone to the harbor?

Iago: Ay, madam.

Desdemona: (To herself, as she continues the amusing conversation to cover up her worry.) I am not merry, but I do beguile the thing I am by seeming otherwise. *(To Iago)* What praise couldst thou bestow on a deserving woman?

Iago: (Describing the perfect woman in a poem—beautiful, quiet, plainly dressed, unselfish, self-controlled, thoughtful, not flirtatious.)

She that was ever fair, and never proud;
Had tongue at will, and yet was never loud;
Never lacked gold, and yet went never "gay";
Fled from her wish, and yet said, "Now I may";
She that being angered, her revenge being nigh,
Bade her wrong stay, and her displeasure fly;
She that could think and ne'er disclose her mind;
See suitors following and not look behind:
She was a wight—if ever such wights were...

Desdemona: To do what?

Iago: *(Dismissing the perfect woman as good only for babies and household accounts.)*

...To suckle fools and chronicle small beer!

(All laugh and applaud, though the women shake their heads.)

Desdemona: O most lame and impotent conclusion! *(With a chuckle to Emelia.)* Do not learn of him, Emilia, though he be thy husband. *(To the young lieutenant.)* How say you, Cassio? Is he not a most profane and liberal counselor?

Cassio: *(He grins at the rough truth of the ensign.)* He speaks home, madam. *(With a shrug, he dismisses Iago as uneducated.)* You may relish him more in the soldier than in the scholar. *(He takes Desdemona's hand gracefully as they stroll off to see the storm die down over the harbor.)*

Iago: *(Stung by Cassio's insult, he mocks the well-mannered behavior of the two young aristocrats.)* He takes her by the palm. *(As Cassio speaks in her ear.)* Ay, well said! Whisper! *(Like a spider he will trap them by twisting fashionable courtesy into a flirtation.)* With as little a web as this will I ensnare as great a fly as Cassio. *(Cassio smiles with delight at Desdemona, as Iago mocks his courtly speech.)* Ay, smile upon her, do! "You say true. Tis so, indeed!"

(Cassio enthusiastically kisses his fingers in the air.) If such tricks as these strip you out of your lieutenantry, it had been better you had not kissed your three fingers so oft...*(Cassio repeats the gesture.)*...which now again you are most apt

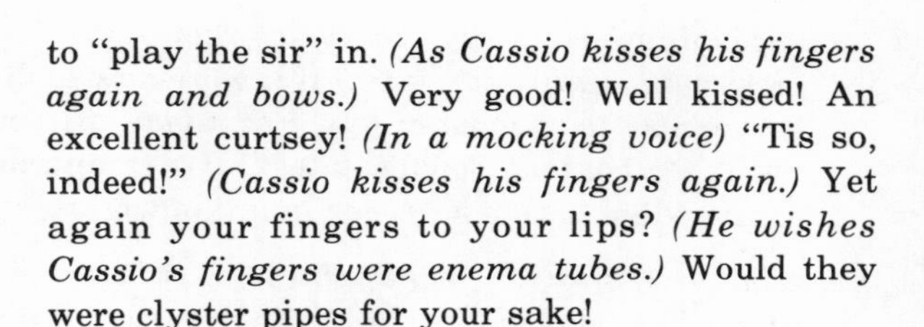

to "play the sir" in. *(As Cassio kisses his fingers again and bows.)* Very good! Well kissed! An excellent curtsey! *(In a mocking voice)* "Tis so, indeed!" *(Cassio kisses his fingers again.)* Yet again your fingers to your lips? *(He wishes Cassio's fingers were enema tubes.)* Would they were clyster pipes for your sake!

(A series of trumpet blasts jar him from his scornful thoughts, and he shouts to the others.) The Moor! I know his trumpet.

Cassio: (Looking off to the harbor.) Tis truly so! *(All shout with joy, and Desdemona is radiant.)*

Desdemona: Let's meet him and receive him!

Cassio: Lo, where he comes!

(To a great burst of trumpets, Othello and his attendants enter. Behind him, the sun breaks through the clouds. For a moment, Othello stands still, overjoyed to see his bride, who has conquered his heart.)

Othello: O, my fair warrior!

Desdemona: (Running lightly to him, her face aglow with love.) My dear Othello!

Othello: It gives me wonder great as my content to see you here before me! *(He seizes her in his arms.)* O, my soul's joy! *(He welcomes storms that have such happy endings.)* If after every tempest come such calms, may the winds blow till they have wakened death, and let the laboring bark climb hills of seas Olympus high, and duck again as low as Hell's from Heaven!

(Grasping her tightly, he knows this is the happiest moment life can give.) If it were now to die, 'twere now to be most happy! For, I fear, my soul hath her content so absolute that not another comfort like to this succeeds in unknown fate!

Desdemona: (A prayer for happiness to enlarge with time.) The heavens forbid but that our loves and comforts should increase, even as our days do grow!

Othello: Amen to that, sweet powers! I cannot speak enough of this content. *(Touching his heart, which has been overcome.)* It stops me here. It is too much of joy! *(With little kisses, he promises they will be the only interruptions to their harmony.)* And this, and this, the greatest discords be that e'er our hearts shall make!

Iago: (Talking to himself) O, you are well-tuned now! *(He plans to un-string their harp of happiness.)* But I'll set down the pegs that make this music, as "honest" as I am.

Othello: (To Desdemona) Come, let us to the castle. *(Raising his hand, he makes a welcome announcement to the others.)* News, friends! Our wars are done! The Turks are drowned! *(Cheers ring out, and Othello turns to his good friend Montano.)* How does my old acquaintance of this isle? *(To Desdemona, sure of her welcome here.)* Honey, you shall be well desired in Cyprus! I have found great love amongst them. *(Another kiss)* O, my sweet! *(To Iago, to collect his private boxes.)* I prithee, good Iago, go to the bay and disembark my coffers. Come, Desdemona! *(To everyone)* Once more, well met at Cyprus!

Othello: If it were now to die, 'twere now to be most happy!

(Amid congratulations, they leave, joyous that their trip has ended, not in war but in a honeymoon. The rest begin to disperse, except for Iago and Roderigo, who has been watching the lovers with a sour face.)

Iago: (To an attendant) Do thou meet me presently at the harbor. *(The man nods and departs, and the ensign turns to Roderigo, inventing lies about Cassio.)* Come hither! The lieutenant tonight watches on the court of guard. First, I must tell thee this: Desdemona is in love with him!

Roderigo: (Shocked) With him? Why, tis not possible!

Iago: Lay thy finger thus...*(He puts his finger to his lips in secrecy)*...and let thy soul be instructed. *(As Roderigo listens reluctantly, Iago spins a web of falsehood.)* Mark me with what violence she first loved the Moor but for bragging and telling her fantastical lies. And will she love him still? Let not thy heart think it!

(When marriage has become old, she will crave handsome new lovers like Cassio.) When the blood is made dull with the act of sport, there should be a game to inflame it—loveliness in favor, sympathy in years, manners and beauties—all which the Moor is defective in. Very nature will compel her to some second choice. Now, sir, this granted—who stands so eminent in the degree of this fortune as Cassio does? Why, none! Why, none! The knave is handsome, young, and the woman hath found him already!

Roderigo: (Unconvinced, as he knows Desdemona's innocent nature.) I cannot believe that in her. She's full of most blessed condition!

Iago: (With a coarse gesture) Blessed fig's end! The wine she drinks is made of grapes. If she had been "blessed," she would never have loved the Moor. Blessed pudding! *(Waving towards the spot where Cassio and Desdemona whispered privately.)* Didst thou not see her paddle with the palm of his hand? Didst not mark that?

Roderigo: Yes, that I did. But that was but courtesy!

Iago: (Insisting it was sex.) Lechery, by this hand! They met so near with their lips that their breaths embraced together. Pish!

(With a plot for Roderigo to start an argument with Cassio, who will then lose his high position.) But, sir, be you ruled by me. I have brought you from Venice. Watch you tonight. Cassio knows you not. I'll not be far from you. Do you find some occasion to anger Cassio, either by speaking too loud, or tainting his discipline, or from what other course you please.

Roderigo: Well...

Iago: Sir, he's rash and very sudden and may strike at you. Provoke him, that he may, for even out of that will I cause the dis-planting of Cassio.

Roderigo: (Selfishly) I will do this, if I can bring it to any opportunity. *(He hopes, with Cassio out of the way, he may have Desdemona yet.)*

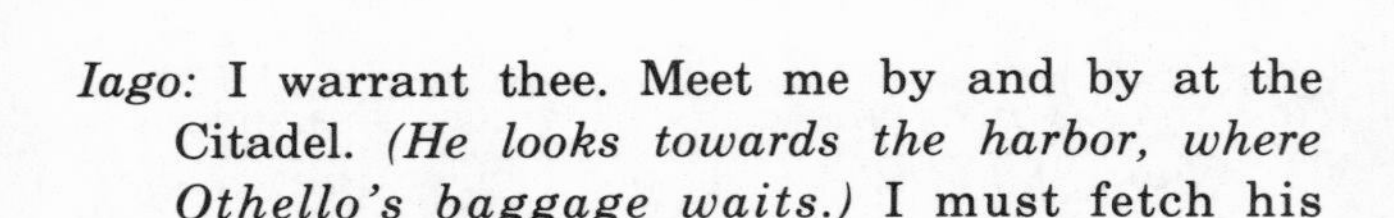

Iago: I warrant thee. Meet me by and by at the Citadel. *(He looks towards the harbor, where Othello's baggage waits.)* I must fetch his necessaries ashore. Farewell!

Roderigo: Adieu. *(He leaves, most unhappy about the developments.)*

Iago: *(To himself, as he plans aloud.)* That Cassio loves her, I do well believe it. *(The false tale of flirtation sounds possible.)* That she loves him, tis apt and of great credit. The Moor is of a constant, loving, noble nature. And I dare think he'll prove to Desdemona a most dear husband.

(With a wicked laugh) Now I do love her too, not out of absolute lust but partly my revenge.

(He will have many rewards for defeating Cassio, as if in a wrestling match.) I'll have our Michael Cassio "on the hip." Make the Moor thank me, love me, and reward me for making him egregiously an ass, and practicing upon his peace and quiet, even to madness! *(Full of schemes against his enemies, he leaves with a light step.)*

Scene 2

(In the late afternoon on the city square, Othello's Herald appears to make an announcement to the people. At the sound of the trumpet, he calls out the news: the city is to celebrate its escape from the Turks and also to cheer Othello's marriage. A sunset glow floods the scene.)

Herald: It is Othello's pleasure, our noble and valiant general, that upon certain tidings now arrived of the Turkish fleet, every man put himself into triumph. Some to dance, some to make bonfires, each man to sport and revel. For, besides these beneficial news, it is the celebration of his nuptial —so much was his pleasure should be proclaimed!

(With a gesture towards the open doors of the city granary, where food and wine are free to all.) All offices are open, and there is full liberty of feasting from this present hour of five till the bell have told eleven. *(The townsfolk cheer.)* Heaven bless the Isle of Cyprus and our noble general Othello! *(As the Herald leaves, the people rush to help themselves to food and wine, shouting their approval.)*

Scene 3

(In the hall of the Citadel or fortress of Cyprus, Othello now wears Montano's gold chain-of-office as governor. While Desdemona and attendants stand nearby, the general gives Cassio orders to post the guard. It is dark, and the soldiers and townsfolk are still celebrating noisily outside.)

Othello: Good Michael, look you to the guard tonight.

Cassio: *(He promises to supervise, although Iago has been delegated the duty.)* Iago hath direction what to do. But notwithstanding, with my personal eye, will I look to it.

Othello: Iago is most honest. Michael, good night. *(They bow in friendship.)* Tomorrow with your earliest, let me have speech with you. *(To his wife)* Come, my dear love! *(Again to Cassio)* Good night! *(As he leaves with Desdemona and the attendants for their rooms, Iago enters from the outer part of the fort.)*

Cassio: Welcome, Iago! We must to the watch.

Iago: (Shaking his head, he slaps Cassio on the arm in a rough, friendly manner.) Not this hour, lieutenant. Tis not yet ten o'clock. *(He looks after Othello and Desdemona with a leer.)* Our general cast us thus early for the love of his Desdemona. He hath not yet "made wanton the night" with her, and she is sport for Jove! *(He bellows with manly laughter.)*

Cassio: (Severely, with great respect.) She's a most exquisite lady.

Iago: (Smacking his lips) And, I'll warrant her, full of game!

Cassio: (With distaste) Indeed, she's a most fresh and delicate creature.

Iago: And when she speaks, is it not an alarum to love? *(He winks and digs Cassio in the ribs with his elbow.)*

Cassio: (In a very proper voice of approval.) She is indeed perfection!

Iago: Well, happiness to their sheets! *(Seeing he cannot make Cassio lust after Desdemona, he changes the subject to drinking companions.)* Come, Lieutenant. I have a stoup of wine! *(He gestures towards a group of noisy men outside.)* And here without are a brace of Cyprus gallants that would fain have a measure to the health of black Othello.

Cassio: Not tonight, good Iago. *(He becomes drunk too easily.)* I have very poor and unhappy brains for drinking. *(With a sigh, he wishes liquor was not a social habit.)* I could well wish courtesy would invent some other entertainment.

Iago: O, they are our friends! But one cup!

Cassio: I have drunk but one cup tonight…*(He looks at his shaky hand, already much affected.)* …and behold what innovation it makes here. *(Refusing more wine)* I am unfortunate in the infirmity and dare not task my weakness with any more.

Iago: What, man! Tis a night of revels! *(He points to the door.)* The gallants desire it!

Cassio: (Tempted) Where are they?

Iago: Here, at the door. I pray you, call them in!

Cassio: I'll do it, but it dislikes me. *(He goes to call in Iago's friends, and the ensign chuckles as he plans to get Cassio as drunk as Roderigo.)*

Iago: If I can fasten but one cup upon him, with that which he hath drunk tonight already, he'll be as full of quarrel and offense as my young mistress' dog. Now my sick fool Roderigo hath tonight caroused "potations pottle-deep!" But here they come!

*Cassio: (Returning with Montano and some gentlemen, all with wine-cups in hand. Cassio waves a *half-empty cup.)* 'Fore God, they have given me a rouse already!

Montano: Good faith, a little one, not past a pint! *(A gentleman fills the cups again, and Iago takes one also.)*

Iago: Some wine, ho! *(He starts a drinking song.)*

And let me the canakin clink, clink.
And let me the canakin clink.
A soldier's a man,
A life's but a span,
Why, then, let a soldier drink!

Cassio: (Applauding as his wine-cup is refilled.) 'Fore God, an excellent song!

Iago: I learned it in England, where indeed they are most potent in "potting." *(All laugh as he tells of English drinking.)* Your Dane, your German, and your swag-bellied Hollander—Drink, ho! . . . *(The gentleman re-fills his cup.)* . . . are nothing to your English!

Cassio: (Raising his shaking cup) To the health of our general!

Montano: I am for it, lieutenant, and I'll do you justice! *(They empty the wine down their throats and hold out the cups for more.)*

Iago: O sweet England! *(He sings a song about a stingy English king.)*

King Stephen was a worthy peer;
His breeches cost him but a crown.
He held them sixpence all too dear,
With that he called the tailor, "Loon!"

He was a wight of high renown,
And thou art but of low degree.
Tis pride that pulls the country down,
And take thine old cloak about thee!

(Holding out his cup) Some wine, ho!

Cassio: (Quite drunk) Why, this is a more exquisite song than the other!

Iago: Will you hear it again? *(He puts his arm around Cassio in the fashion of drinking comrades. Cassio looks at it, shakes the arm off, and suddenly tries to be sober.)*

Cassio: (With deep disapproval) No, for I hold him to be unworthy of his place that does those things! *(Making a speech on religion.)* Well, God's above all, and there be souls must be saved, and there be souls must not be saved. *(He hiccups in a dignified manner.)*

Iago: (Filling Cassio's wine cup again.) It's true, good lieutenant.

Cassio: (Taking a very formal swallow of wine.) For mine own part—no offense—I hope to be saved.

Iago: And so do I too, lieutenant!

Cassio: (Insisting on the priority of his rank.) Aye, but, by your leave, not before me. The lieutenant is to be saved before the ancient. *(He hiccups again.)* Let's have no more of this. *(He stands, prepared to oversee the watchmen.)* Let's to our affairs. *(Crossing himself)* God forgive us our sins! Gentlemen, let's look to our business.

(He belches. The others laugh drunkenly, and Cassio takes offense.) Do not think, gentlemen, I am drunk! *(Carefully he identifies Iago.)* This is my ancient. *(He stares at his left hand.)* This is my right hand. *(Then he stares at his right.)* And this is my left! I am not drunk now! *(He takes a step and almost loses his balance.)* I can stand well enough and speak well enough!

All: Excellent well!

Cassio: Why, very well, then. You must not think then that I am drunk! *(Very erect, he staggers off towards the battlements. The others follow, laughing.)*

Montano: To the platform, masters! Come, let's set the watch.

Iago: (Lagging behind, he catches Montano by the sleeve and points after Cassio.) You see this fellow that is gone before? *(Montano nods.)* He is a soldier fit to stand by Caesar and give direction. And do but see his vice! *(Montano's eyes open wide—Cassio is a drunkard!—and he nods with understanding.)*

Montano: But is he often thus?

Iago: (Swearing that Cassio is drunk every night.) Tis evermore the prologue to his sleep.

Montano: It were well the general were put in mind of it. *(Worried, he starts towards the door to Othello's chambers. Unseen by him, Roderigo enters drunk, and Iago gives the fool secret directions.)*

Iago: How now, Roderigo? I pray you, after the lieutenant, go! *(He pushes Roderigo off as Montano turns, reluctant to disturb the honeymoon couple, and repeats his statement.)*

Montano: It were an honest action to say so to the Moor.

Iago: Not I, for this fair island! I do love Cassio well and would do much to cure him of this evil. But hark! What noise?

Voices: (From the watchtower of the fort.) Help! Help!

(Cassio enters, pursuing Roderigo in a drunken fury.)

Cassio: Zounds, you rogue! You rascal! *(He beats the fool with the flat of his sword.)*

Montano: (Trying to stop the fight.) What's the matter, lieutenant?

Cassio: A knave teach me my duty? I'll beat the knave into a bottle! *(He chases Roderigo about the hall, slashing at him.)*

Roderigo: Beat me? *(From behind Iago's back, he sticks out his tongue at Cassio.)*

Cassio: Dost thou prate, rogue? *(He strikes again at Roderigo.)*

Montano: Nay, good lieutenant! *(He holds Cassio's arms.)* I pray you, sir, hold your hold your hand.

Cassio: Let me go, sir, or I'll knock you! *(He struggles to be free.)*

Montano: Come, come, you're drunk!

Cassio: Drunk? *(With a roar, he attacks Montano with sword and dagger. Montano draws his own weapons, and Iago pushes Roderigo to the outer door.)*

Iago: Away, I say. Go out and cry a mutiny! *(Now half-sober, Roderigo nods and slips outside. Iago returns, pretending to stop the fight.)* Nay, good lieutenant. God's will, gentlemen! Help, ho! Lieutenant! Sir! Montano! Sir! *(Shouting loudly to make matters worse.)* Help, masters! Here's a goodly watch indeed! *(An alarm bell rings.)* Who's that which rings the bell?

(As Montano and Cassio circle each other, exchanging thrusts and parries, Iago overturns furniture behind their backs.) Diablo, ho! The town will rise! *(Unnoticed by the fighters, he throws a wine jar through the window and shouts as it smashes.)* God's will, lieutenant, hold! You will be shamed forever! *(With his sword he strikes first one and then the other man unnoticed, until Othello and his attendants enter. At this point, Iago becomes an innocent bystander.)*

Othello: What is the matter here?

Montano: (Looking at a bad wound.) Zounds, I bleed still! I am hurt to the death. *(In a rage at Cassio.)* He dies! *(They fight even more furiously, while Iago attempts to separate them.)*

Othello: Hold, for your lives! *(He motions to his guards to help Iago.)*

Iago: Hold, ho! Lieutenant . . . Sir! . . . Montano! . . . Gentlemen! . . . Have you forgot all place of sense and duty?...Hold!...The general speaks to you!...Hold, hold, for shame! *(But the sword-fight continues while attendants try to stop it, and the alarm bell clangs outside.)*

Othello: Why, how now, ho! From whence ariseth this? Are we turned Turks? For Christian shame, put by this barbarous brawl! He that stirs next, he dies upon his motion. *(To a gentleman)* Silence that dreadful bell! It frights the isle. *(As the gentleman leaves, the two fighters, separated, come to their senses. Bewildered, they kneel for forgiveness.)* What is the matter, masters? *(To his ensign, who seems overcome with sorrow.)* Honest Iago, that looks dead with grieving, speak! Who began this?

Iago: (Avoiding a direct answer) I do not know. Friends all, but now, even now. And then, but now...swords out and tilting one at other's breast in opposition bloody. I cannot speak any beginning to this.

Othello: (To Cassio) How comes it, Michael?

Cassio: (Full of shame) I pray you, pardon me. I cannot speak.

Othello: Worthy Montano, the gravity and stillness of your youth the world hath noted. And your name is great. Give me answer for it!

Montano: (Holding his injured arm) Worthy Othello, I am hurt to danger! Your officer, Iago, can inform you.

Othello: (Furious that no one will tell him what happened.) Now, by Heaven, my blood begins my safer guides to rule! *(To all)* Give me to know how this foul rout began. Who set it on? What? In a town of war, yet wild, the people's hearts brimful of fear, to quarrel? In night and on the court and guard of safety? Tis monstrous! *(Turning to Iago again)* Iago, who began it?

Iago: (Sadly) Thus it is, general. Montano and myself being in speech, there comes a fellow crying out for help, and Cassio following him with determined sword. *(Indicating Montano)* Sir, this gentleman steps in to Cassio and entreats his pause. Myself the crying fellow did pursue. He, swift of foot, outran my purpose. When I came back—for this was brief—I found them close together...*(He points to Cassio and Montano.)* ...at blow and thrust. More of this matter cannot I report. *(He shrugs as he hunts for an apology.)* But men are men! The best sometimes forget.

Othello: I know, Iago. *(He motions his lieutenant forward and, before all the others, dismisses him from service.)* Cassio, I love thee. But never more be officer of mine!

(Cassio almost faints from shame. Desdemona, with her women, enters to see what has happened.) Look if my gentle love be not raised up! *(To Cassio, sternly)* I'll make thee an example!

Desdemona: What's the matter?

Othello: (Tenderly) All's well now, sweeting. Come away to bed. *(To Montano)* Sir, for your hurts, myself will be your surgeon. *(To the others)* Lead him off. *(Montano is taken to Othello's rooms as*

the general turns to his ensign.) Iago, look with care about the town, and silence those whom this vile brawl distracted. *(To his bride)* Come, Desdemona. *(With a wry smile of apology.)* Tis the soldiers' life to have their balmy slumbers waked with strife.

(All leave but Iago and Cassio, who sits silent, his head in his hands.)

Iago: What, are you hurt, lieutenant? *(He uses the former title mockingly, but Cassio is too downcast to notice.)*

Cassio: Ay, past all surgery.

Iago: Marry, Heaven forbid!

Cassio: Reputation, reputation, reputation! O, I have lost my reputation! I have lost the immortal part of myself...*(He looks at his body as if at an animal.)*...and what remains is bestial. My reputation, Iago! My reputation! *(He groans and hold his head again in despair.)*

Iago: As I am an honest man, I thought you had received some bodily wound. *(He jokes at reputation, which is only a surface impression to him, easily gained and lost.)* Reputation is an idle and most false imposition, oft got without merit and lost without deserving. *(All depends on what Cassio believes.)* You have lost no reputation at all unless you repute yourself such a loser.

(He cheers Cassio with thoughts of being forgiven after Othello's mood changes.) What, man, there are more ways to recover the general again.

You are but now "cast in his mood." *(He encourages Cassio to plead his case.)* Sue to him again, and he's yours!

Cassio: (Full of guilt) I will rather sue to be despised than to deceive so good a commander with so slight, so drunken and so indiscreet an officer! Drunk? And squabble? Swagger? Swear? *(With a curse at alcohol.)* O thou invisible spirit of wine, if thou hast no name to be known by, let us call thee, "Devil"! O God, that men should put an enemy in their mouths, to steal away their brains! *(He hates the changes wine makes in him.)* To be now a sensible man, by and by a fool, and presently a beast! O . . . strange!

Iago: Come, come, good wine is a good familiar creature, if it be well used.

Cassio: (Shuddering at his memories) I . . . drunk?

Iago: You or any man living may be drunk at a time, man. I'll tell you what you shall do. *(Cassio looks up, beginning to hope at the honest tone of Iago's rough voice.)* Our general's wife is now the general. Confess yourself freely to her! *(Desdemona, as a good general's wife, will surely help poor Cassio.)* Importune her help to put you in your place again. She is of so free, so kind, so apt, so blessed a disposition, she holds it a vice in her goodness not to do more than she is requested.

Cassio: You advise me well!

Iago: (With a hand on his "honest" heart.) I protest, in the sincerity of love and honest kindness!

Cassio: Betimes in the morning I will beseech the virtuous Desdemona to undertake for me. I am desperate of my fortunes!

Iago: You are in the right! Good night, lieutenant. I must to the watch.

Cassio: Good night, honest Iago! *(He leaves, looking a little hopeful.)*

Iago: (Laughing at himself, for being so much help.) And what's he then that says I play the villain, when this advice is free I give, and honest, and indeed the course to win the Moor again. How am I then a villain? *(He laughs, knowing Evil works best by pretending to be Good, and so will Iago.)* When devils will the blackest sins put on, they do suggest at first with heavenly shows, as I do now.

(When Cassio asks Desdemona to plead with Othello, Iago will poison the general's mind, so that Desdemona will seem to plead for her lover. The more she asks, the worse she will seem.) For whiles this honest fool plies Desdemona to repair his fortune, and she for him pleads strongly to the Moor, I'll pour this pestilence into his ear—that she repeals him for her body's lust! And by how much she strives to do him good, she shall un-do her credit with the Moor. So will I turn her virtue into pitch! *(His delighted malice is interrupted by Roderigo, who enters, most unhappy.)* How now, Roderigo?

Roderigo: My money is almost spent! *(He feels his bruises from the fight with Cassio.)* I have been tonight exceedingly well cudgeled. And I think the issue will be I shall have so much experience for my pains. And so, with no money at all and a little more wit, return again to Venice!

Iago: (Scolding) How poor are they that have not patience! What wound did ever heal but by degrees? *(Cleverness always take time.)* Thou knowst we work by wit, and not by witchcraft, and wit depends on dilatory time. *(Showing their progress so far.)* Does it not go well? Cassio hath beaten thee, and thou by that small hurt hath cashiered Cassio. *(Roderigo brightens to hear of Cassio's dismissal.)* Content thyself awhile!

(As he speaks, the dawn begins to break.) By the mass, tis morning. Pleasure and action make the hours seem short! *(Pushing Roderigo towards his bed.)* Retire thee. Nay, get thee gone! *(The fool stumbles off sleepily.)*

(Iago, refreshed by his success, begins his plans. Emilia must help Cassio see Desdemona. And Iago must make Othello suspect that Cassio and Desdemona are lovers by showing them together.) Two things are to be done. My wife must move for Cassio to her mistress. I'll set her on. Myself awhile to draw the Moor apart and bring him jump when he may Cassio find soliciting his wife. *(He rubs his hands together in glee.)* Ay, that's the way! *(Briskly deciding to strike while the iron is hot.)* Dull not device by coldness and delay! *(He skips off, breaking into clumsy little dance steps.)*

ACT III

Scene 1

(In mid-morning of the same day, in a street next to the Citadel, Cassio approaches a servant. He wants to bribe his way to see Emilia and eventually Desdemona, but he stands uncertain how to begin. Finally he clears his throat. The clownish servant makes no response.)

Cassio: Dost thou hear, my honest friend?

Clown: No, I hear not your honest friend. I hear **you.**

Cassio: *(Pressing a coin into his hand.)* There's a poor piece of gold for thee. If the gentlewoman that attends the general's wife be stirring, tell her there's one Cassio entreats her a little favor of speech. Wilt thou do this?

Clown: She is stirring, sir. *(He mocks Cassio's overly fancy speech.)* If she will stir hither, I shall seem to notify unto her. *(He enters the fortress, imitating Cassio's graceful walk. At the same time, from the opposite direction comes Iago. Cassio greets him as a friend.)*

Cassio: In happy time, Iago!

Iago: You have not been abed then?

Cassio: Why, no. The day had broke before we parted. I have made bold, Iago, to send in to your wife. My suit to her is that she will to virtuous Desdemona procure me some access.

Iago: I'll send her to you presently. *(To help matters, he will make sure Othello is gone while Cassio speaks to Desdemona.)* And I'll devise a mean to draw the Moor out of the way, that your converse and business may be more free.

Cassio: I humbly thank you for it. *(With gratitude, he watches Iago enter the Citadel.)* I never knew a Florentine more kind and honest!

(Emilia comes from the Citadel, a look of sympathy on her pleasant face.)

Emilia: Good morrow, good lieutenant. I am sorry for your displeasure, but all will sure be well.

Cassio: Yet, I beseech you, if you think fit or that it may be done, give me advantage of some brief discourse with Desdemona alone.

Emilia: (Kindly) Pray you come in.

Cassio: I am much bound to you. *(They leave to meet Desdemona in private.)*

Scene 2

(In Othello's office, he sends reports to Venice before going to inspect the earthwork walls and other fortifications of the island with his staff. The general hands Iago a package of mail.)

Othello: These letters give, Iago, to the pilot, and by him do my duties to the Senate. That done, I will be walking on the "works." Repair there to me.

Iago: Well, my good lord, I'll do it.

Othello: (To the others) This fortification, gentlemen ... shall we see it?

Gentleman: We'll wait upon your lordship. *(Attended by his escort, the general leaves the Citadel.)*

Scene 3

(In the garden of the castle, Desdemona promises to plead Cassio's cause, as being an unofficial counselor is one of the customary duties of a ruler's wife.)

Desdemona: Be thou assured, good Cassio, I will do all my abilities in thy behalf!

Emilia: Good madam, do! *(She imagines that Iago, too, is unhappy.)* I warrant it grieves my husband as if the case were his.

Desdemona: (With approval of the rough-spoken man.) O, that's an honest fellow! *(To the young officer)* Do not doubt, Cassio, but I will have my lord and you again as friendly as you were.

Cassio: (Kneeling in thanks) Bounteous madam, whatever shall become of Michael Cassio, he's never anything but your true servant!

Desdemona: I know it. I thank you. You do love my lord. You have known him long. *(Holding up her hand in an oath.)* Assure thee, if I do vow a friendship, I'll perform it to the last article! *(Almost mischievously, she tells the various ways she will plead for him, even to death.)* My lord shall never rest...I'll talk him out of patience ...His bed shall seem a school...I'll intermingle everything he does with Cassio's suit. Therefore be merry, Cassio! For thy solicitor shall rather die than give thy cause away! *(Cassio, still kneeling, takes Desdemona's hand and covers it with extravagant yet sincere kisses of gratitude.)*

(At a distance, Othello and Iago enter from the Citadel, conferring about some papers they hold. Seeing them, Cassio drops Desdemona's hand and rises, awkward and embarrased.)

Cassio: Madam, I'll take my leave! *(He starts towards the rear gate.)*

Desdemona: Why, stay, and hear me speak.

Cassio: (Ashamed to meet Othello so soon.) Madam, not now! I am very ill at ease.

Desdemona: Well, do your discretion. *(Cassio bows and almost runs away. Across the garden, Iago, seizing his opportunity, scowls as if something suspicious has happened.)*

Iago: Ha! I like not that!

Othello: What dost thou say? *(He looks at him sharply.)*

Iago: (Too hastily) Nothing, my lord! Or if...I know not what.

Othello: (In an odd tone, pointing towards the women.) Was not that Cassio parted from my wife?

Iago: Cassio, my lord? *(Too eagerly)* No, sure, I cannot think it, that he would steal away so guilty-like, seeing your coming.

Othello: I do believe 'twas he.

Desdemona: (Coming to them, she curtsies and smiles at Othello as she speaks of Cassio and his problem.) How now, my lord? I have been talking with a suitor here, a man that languishes in your displeasure.

Othello: Who is it you mean?

Desdemona: Why, your lieutenant, Cassio.

Othello: Went he hence now?

Desdemona: (Nodding agreement) Ay, sooth, so humbled that he hath left part of his grief with me. Good love, call him back!

Othello: Not now, sweet Desdemona. Some other time. *(He looks at the papers he holds.)*

Desdemona: Shall it be tonight at supper?

Othello: (Shaking his head gravely) No, not tonight.

Desdemona: Tomorrow dinner then?

Othello: I shall not dine at home. I meet the captains at the Citadel.

Desdemona: (As she nags him sweetly to forgive Cassio soon, Othello begins to smile.) Why then, tomorrow night? Or Tuesday morn? On Tuesday noon or night? On Wednesday morn? I prithee, name the time, but let it not exceed three days! *(She knows Cassio is truly sorry.)* In faith, he's penitent! *(Othello merely smiles more as she tugs his gold chain.)* When shall he come? *(He laughs.)* Tell me, Othello! I wonder in my soul what you would ask me that I should stand so mammering on! *(He takes her in his arms and kisses her, but she continues speaking.)* What, Michael Cassio, that came a-wooing with you, to have so much to do to bring him in? Trust me, I could do much...

Othello: (Stopping her with kisses) Prithee, no more. Let him come when he will! I will deny thee nothing! *(Iago turns away frustrated, as Othello continues to his wife.)* Whereon I do beseech thee, grant me this—to leave me but a little to myself!

Desdemona: (Giving him a great hug.) Shall I deny you? No! Farewell, my lord.

Othello: Farewell, my Desdemona. I'll come to thee straight.

Desdemona: Emilia, come. *(To her husband, with a dutiful curtsey.)* Whatever you be, I am obedient. *(The two women leave, whispering happily.)*

Othello: (Watching them go, he sighs with love.) Excellent wretch! Perdition catch my soul but I do love thee! And when I love thee not, Chaos is come again.

Iago: My noble lord....

Othello: What dost thou say, Iago?

Iago: Did Michael Cassio, when you wooed my lady, know of your love?

Othello: He did, from first to last.

Iago: *(Frowning as if at a horrible secret thought.)* Indeed?

Othello: *(Imitating him)* "Indeed?" Ay, indeed! *(Troubled)* Is he not honest?

Iago: *(Not answering directly)* Honest, my lord?

Othello: Honest? Ay, honest.

Iago: *(Giving a half-answer)* My lord, for aught I know....

Othello: *(Puzzled at the evasive answers from his usually outspoken officer.)* What dost thou think?

Iago: Think, my lord?

Othello: *(Irritated at the repetitions)* "Think, my lord?" By Heaven, he echoes me as if there were some monster in his thought too hideous to be shown! *(Iago turns away, and Othello takes him by the shoulders, turns him back again and looks him squarely in the face.)* Thou dost mean something!

(Pointing towards the place where Cassio spoke to Desdemona.) I heard thee say, even now, thou likest not that when Cassio left my wife. What didst not like?

(Iago turns his face aside and looks at the ground, silent. Othello grips his face and turns it up again, growing more disturbed.) And when I

told thee he was of my counsel in my whole course of wooing, thou criedst, "Indeed?" and didst contract and purse thy brow together as if thou then hadst shut up in thy brain some horrible conceit.

(Slowly he voices his demand.) If thou dost love me, show . . . me . . . thy . . . thought!

Iago: (After a long pause, he says carefully.) For Michael Cassio, I dare be sworn, I think that he is honest.

Othello: (Confidently) I think so too!

Iago: (Almost to himself) Men should be what they seem . . . .

Othello: Certain, men should be what they seem!

Iago: (With peculiar emphasis) Why then, I "think" Cassio's an honest man . . . .

Othello: (Confused and angry) Nay, yet there's more in this? I prithee, speak to me as to thy "thinkings," and give thy worst of thoughts the worst of words.

Iago: (Suddenly breaking away with a declaration that he is free to be silent.) Good my lord, pardon me! Though I am bound to every act of duty, I am not bound to that all slaves are free to. *(His thoughts might be wrong.)* Utter my thoughts? Why, say they are vile and false. *(Hinting of desperate trouble)* It were not for your quiet nor your good, nor for my manhood, honesty or wisdom, to let you know my thoughts!

Othello: (A roar of suspicion) What dost thou mean?

Iago: O beware, my lord, of jealousy! It is the green-eyed monster.

Iago: (With a saintly air, he refuses to risk any precious reputation by spreading gossip.) "Good name" in man and woman, dear my lord, is the immediate jewel of their souls. *(It is more dear than gold.)* Who steals my purse steals trash: tis something ... nothing. 'Twas mine, tis his, and has been slave to thousands. But he that filches from me my "good name," robs me of that which not en-riches him and makes me poor indeed!

Othello: By Heaven, I'll know thy thoughts! *(He seizes Iago by the arm.)*

Iago: (Simply) You cannot, if my heart were in your hand.

Othello: Ha! *(Baffled by the complications of human nature, so different from the simple life of battle, he lets go of Iago's arm and sits heavily on a garden bench. Iago moves behind him, hinting of trouble.)*

Iago: O beware, my lord, of jealousy! It is the green-eyed monster, which doth mock the meat it feeds on. *(Othello slowly freezes as Iago tells him of happy but betrayed husbands, cuckolds, who know the truth, and of unhappy cuckolds who merely guess.)* That cuckold lives in bliss who, certain of his fate, loves not his wronger. But O, what damned minutes tells he o'er ... who dotes, yet doubts, ... suspects, yet strongly loves!

Othello: (The message of an unfaithful wife strikes him.) O misery!

Iago: (A warning against worry) Poor and content is rich, and rich enough. But riches is as poor as winter to him that ever fears he shall be poor. Good Heaven, the souls of all my tribe defend from jealousy!

Othello: Why? Why is this? Thinkst thou I'd make a life of jealousy, to follow still the changes of the moon with fresh suspicions? No! *(With simple logic, he would prove any suspicion or forget it.)* To be once in doubt is once to be resolved. *(But mere social talents would not make him suspect his wife.)* Tis not to make me jealous to say my wife is fair, feeds well, loves company, is free of speech, sings, plays, and dances well. Where virtue is, these are more virtuous. She had eyes... and chose me!

No, Iago. I'll see before I doubt. When I doubt, prove. *(With proof, he will make a direct choice.)* And on the proof there is no more but this: away at once with love or jealousy!

Iago: (Expressing relief that he can speak openly to Othello's good judgment, he sits beside his general.) I am glad of it! For now I shall have reason to show the love and duty that I bear you with franker spirit. Therefore, as I am bound, receive it from me. I speak not yet of "proof."

(With a crude hint) Look to your wife! Observe her well with Cassio. *(As Othello glares at the gate where Cassio left so hurriedly, Iago urges him to be neither suspicious nor certain.)* Wear your eye thus: not jealous nor secure. I would not have your free and noble nature be abused. Look to it!

(Iago whispers of secret adulteries in Venice.) I know our country disposition well. In Venice they

do let Heaven see the pranks they dare not show their husbands. Their best conscience is not to "leave un-done," but "keep unknown!"

Othello: (Appalled, for he knows little of city life.) Dost thou say so?

Iago: (Pointing out her past dishonesties.) She did deceive her father, marrying you. And when she seemed to shake and fear your looks, she loved them most.

Othello: And so she did!

Iago: Why, go to, then. *(Her father was especially misled.)* She that, so young, could give out such a "seeming," he thought 'twas witchcraft! *(Othello moans as if remembering Brabantio's warning: she had deceived her father and might do the same for her husband! Iago sees Othello's face reflect his suspicions.)* But I am much to blame. I humbly do beseech you of your pardon for too much loving you!

Othello: I am bound to thee forever!

Iago: I see this hath a little dashed your spirits.

Othello: (Tight-lipped) Not a jot, not a jot.

Iago: In faith, I fear it has. I hope you will consider what is spoke comes from my love. *(Othello turns aside to hide his mounting jealousy.)* But I do see you are moved. *(He slaps him on the shoulder in heartiness.)* I pray you not to strain my speech to grosser issues nor to larger reach than to "suspicion."

Othello: I will not.

Iago: Cassio's my worthy friend... *(Othello's eyes fill with tears.)* My lord, I see you are moved.

Othello: No, not much moved. *(He wipes his eyes roughly on his sleeve and his voice shakes.)* I do not think but Desdemona's honest!

Iago: Long live she so! And long live you to "think" so.

Othello: *(Still, he knows the world is flawed.)* And yet, how Nature, erring from itself...

Iago: *(Eagerly agreeing, as he hints that Desdemona, who refused her natural choices, the young men at home, has strange sexual tastes.)* Ay, there's the point, as—to be bold with you—not to affect many proposed matches of her own clime, complexion and degree, whereto we see in all things Nature tends...Foh! One may smell in such... a will most rank, foul disproportion, thoughts un-natural! *(Othello, startled, looks at his black skin and feels his face for wrinkles.)* But pardon me, I do not distinctly speak of her.

(But he warns Desdemona may regret her choice later, comparing Othello to Venetians.) Though I may fear her will, recoiling to her better judgment, may match you with her country forms and happily repent.

Othello: *(Trembling with shock)* Farewell, farewell! If more thou dost perceive, let me know more. Set on thy wife to observe. *(His voice becomes a roar.)* Leave me, Iago!

Iago: My lord, I take my leave. *(He strides out, grinning with success.)*

Othello: Why did I marry? *(He looks after Iago.)* This honest creature doubtless sees and knows more, much more, than he unfolds!

(So sure of himself in the world of war, the great African is helpless in the unfamiliar world of love. He can only trust his old military friend. Savagely, he clasps and unclasps his strong hands, as the tide of jealousy possesses him. Iago returns, confident he has found Othello's weakness, and he makes matters worse by trying to smooth over the problem.)

Iago: My lord, I would I might entreat your honor to scan this thing no further. Leave it to time. *(He suggests Cassio be kept from office a little longer, to observe Desdemona's pleading.)* Although tis fit that Cassio have his place—for, sure, he fills it up with great ability—yet, if you please to hold him off awhile, you shall, by that, perceive him and his means. Note if your lady strain his entertainment with any strong importunity. Much will be seen in that. *(With an apology to the agitated Moor for worrying him too much.)* In the meantime, let me be thought too busy in my fears, and hold her free, I do beseech your honor!

Othello: (Struggling hard for self-control) Fear not my government!

Iago: I once more take my leave. *(With a bow he is gone.)*

Othello: (Looking after him) This fellow's of exceeding honesty! *(If Desdemona turns out to be a half-wild hawk, he will loose her ties.)* If I do prove her haggard, though that her jesses were my dear heart-strings, I'd whistle her off and let her down the wind to prey at fortune.

(He thinks perhaps, because of his color, his lack of social talk, his age, he has lost her.) Haply for I am black and have not those soft parts of conversation that chamberers have, or for I am declined into the vale of years—yet that's not much—she's gone! I am abused! *(All he can do is hate her.)* And my relief must be to loathe her! *(He gives a great cry.)* O curse of marriage, that we can call these delicate creatures ours, and not their appetites!

(Desdemona and Emilia enter.) Desdemona comes! *(He sees her innocent eyes widen with love for him.)* If she be false, O, then Heaven mocks itself! *(He tries to put down his suspicions.)* I'll not believe it!

Desdemona: How now, my dear Othello? *(She gestures back to the banqueting hall where guests await them.)* Your dinner and the generous islanders by you invited do attend your presence.

Othello: (Softly) I am to blame.

Desdemona: Why do you speak so faintly? Are you not well?

Othello: (With a bitter joke, for betrayed husbands were said to wear horns.) I have a pain upon my forehead, here. *(He touches two places.)*

Desdemona: Faith, that's with watching. 'Twill away again. Let me but bind it hard. Within this hour, it will be well! *(She takes a pretty handkerchief embroidered with strawberries from her pocket and tries to tie it about his head to stop the ache.)*

Othello: Your napkin is too little. Let it alone. *(He pushes the handkerchief away, and it falls to the ground unnoticed.)* Come, I'll go in with you.

Desdemona: I am very sorry that you are not well! *(As they leave, he walks stiffly, holding in his runaway emotions. Emilia, following them, spies the fallen handkerchief, which she picks up.)*

Emilia: I am glad I have found this napkin. This was her first remembrance from the Moor. My wayward husband hath a hundred times wooed me to steal it. But she so loves the token that she reserves it evermore about her, to kiss and talk to. *(Planning to have it copied before she gives it to her husband.)* I'll have the work "taken out" and give it Iago. What he will do with it, Heaven knows, not I. *(She tucks it down the front of her dress as Iago returns.)*

Iago: (With a suspicious look about the garden.) How now? What do you here alone?

Emilia: (Refusing to be scolded) Do not you chide. I have a . . . thing . . . for you! What will you give me now for that same handkerchief?

Iago: What handkerchief?

Emilia: What handkerchief? Why, that the Moor first gave to Desdemona.

Iago: (Eagerly) Hast stolen it from her?

Emilia: No, faith, she let it drop by negligence. I, being here, took it up. *(She whisks it out and dangles it before his eyes.)* Look, here it is!

Iago: A good wench! Give it me.

Emilia: (Holding it just beyond his reach, teasing.) What will you do with it, that you have been so earnest to have me filch it?

Iago: Why, what's that to you? *(He snatches it from her hand roughly.)*

Emilia: (Changing her mind) If it be not for some purpose, give it me again! Poor lady, she'll run mad when she shall lack it.

Iago: I have use for it. Go, leave me! *(Emilia exits, already having regrets, but Iago wastes no time making plans.)* I will in Cassio's lodging lose this napkin and let him find it. This may do something. The Moor already changes with my poison. *(Othello enters, and Iago chuckles, amused that now all the sleeping potions in the world will not give him peace.)* Look where he comes! Not poppy nor mandragora, nor all the drowsy syrups of the world, shall ever medicine thee to that sweet sleep which thou ownst yesterday. *(He hides the handkerchief.)*

Othello: (To himself) Ha! Ha! False to me?

Iago: (Strolling over in friendly fashion.) Why, how now, General? *(Othello gives him a stricken look of hate, as if seeing a torturer.)*

Othello: Avaunt! Be gone! Thou hast set me on the rack.

Iago: How now, my lord? *(His "honest" face seems puzzled.)*

Othello: (Eaten up with jealousy) What sense had I of her stolen hours of lust? I saw it not, thought it not. It harmed not me! I slept the next night well, was free and merry. I found not Cassio's kisses on her lips. *(Wishing he did not know the truth.)* He that is robbed, not wanting what is stolen, let him not know it, and he's not robbed at all!

Iago: I am sorry to hear this!

Othello: I had been happy if the general camp, pioners and all, had tasted her sweet body, so I had nothing known!

(Ready for death from sorrow, he bids farewell to life and all its glories.) O now, forever farewell the tranquil mind! Farewell, content! Farewell the plumed troop, and the big wars that make ambition virtue. O, farewell! Farewell the neighing steed and the shrill trump, the spirit-stirring drum, the ear-piercing fife, the royal banner, and all quality, pride, pomp and circumstance of glorious war! *(Even the thundering cannon he will leave.)* And O, you mortal engines whose rude throats the Immortal Jove's dread clamors counterfeit, farewell! Othello's occupation's gone!

Iago: Is it possible, my lord?

Othello: (Turning on him with a threat.) Villain, be sure thou **prove** my love a whore! Be sure of it!

Make me see it...or woe upon thy life! *(He advances to attack Iago with his great hands. Iago backs away.)*

Iago: My noble lord...

Othello: (Choking him as he threatens.) If thou dost slander her and torture me, never pray more! *(Babbling as his grief grows greater.)* On horror's head, horrors accumulate, do deeds to make Heaven weep, all Earth amazed.

Iago: (Breaking away) O grace! O Heaven forgive me! *(He offers to resign, if honesty is rewarded in this fashion.)* Take mine office. O monstrous world! Take note, take note, O world, to be direct and honest is not safe! From hence I'll love no friend.

Othello: (Regretting his attack) Nay, stay! *(Convinced Iago is truthful)* Thou shouldst be honest.

Iago: (Feeling his bruised neck with regret.) I should be wise. For honesty's a fool!

Othello: By the world, I think my wife be honest, and think she is not. I think that thou art just, and think thou art not! *(In an agony of suspicion.)* I'll have some proof. Would I were satisfied!

Iago: I see, sir, you are eaten up with passion. I do repent me that I put it to you! You would be satisfied?

Othello: Would? Nay, and I will!

Iago: And may. But how? How satisfied, my lord? Would you behold her "topped"?

Othello: (Turning away in revulsion.) Death and damnation! O!

Iago: What then? Where's satisfaction? It is impossible you should see this, were they as prime as goats, as hot as monkeys. *(Still, circumstantial evidence is possible.)* But yet, I say, if strong circumstances which lead directly to the door of truth will give you satisfaction, you might have it.

Othello: Give me a living reason she's . . . disloyal!

Iago: (With a ready lie about Cassio talking in his sleep.) I lay with Cassio lately, and being troubled with a raging tooth, I could not sleep. There are a kind of men so loose of soul that in their sleeps will mutter their affairs. One of this kind is Cassio.

In sleep I heard him say, "Sweet Desdemona, let us hide our loves!" And then, sir, would he grip and wring my hand, cry, "O sweet creature!" *(Othello holds his head and moans. Iago rapidly makes the lie even worse.)* And then kiss me hard, as if he plucked up kisses by the roots that grew upon my lips. Then laid his leg over my thigh, and sighed, and kissed, and then cried, "Cursed fate that gave thee to the Moor!"

Othello: O monstrous! Monstrous! *(His control shatters.)*

Iago: Nay, this was but his **dream.**

Othello: But this denoted a foregone conclusion. *(At the edge of madness.)* I'll tear her all to pieces!

Iago: Nay, but be wise. Yet we see nothing done. She may be honest yet!

(Othello shakes his head in hopelessness. Sweaty with success, Iago wipes his brow with a handkerchief. To his surprise, it is Desdemona's. He whips a look to see if Othello has noticed, but the Moor is staring at the ground. As Iago hastily thrusts the handkerchief back into his doublet, he has a new idea.)

Tell me but this: have you not sometimes seen a handkerchief spotted with strawberries in your wife's hand?

Othello: I gave her such a one. 'Twas my first gift.

Iago: I know not that. But such a handkerchief—I am sure it was your wife's—did I today see Cassio wipe his beard with.

Othello: If it be that...

Iago: If it be that, it speaks against her with the other proofs!

Othello: (With primitive justice, he can think only of death as punishment, killing Desdemona many times.) O, that the slave had forty thousand lives! One is too poor, too weak for my revenge. Look here, Iago...*(He gives a great cry of anger to the skies.)*...all my fond love thus do I blow to Heaven! Tis gone! *(He looks downward for help.)* Arise, black Vengeance, from the hollow Hell!

Iago: (Weakly trying to calm him.) Yet, be content.

Othello: O, blood, blood, blood!

Iago: Patience, I say. Your mind perhaps may change!

Othello: Never, Iago! *(As the great currents of the sea, his revenge will not be stopped.)* Like to the Pontic Sea, whose icy current and compulsive course ne'er feels retiring ebb but keeps due on to the Propontic and the Hellespont, even so my bloody thoughts, with violent pace, shall ne'er look back, ne'er ebb to humble love, till that a capable and wide revenge swallow them up!

(He kneels to take a vow of vengeance against Desdemona.) Now, by yond marble Heaven, in the due reverence of a sacred vow, I here engage my words!

Iago: Do not rise yet. *(Iago kneels beside him, swearing revenge also to the skies.)* Witness, you ever-burning lights above, witness that here Iago doth give up his wit, hands, heart to wronged Othello's service! Let him command! *(For a moment they kneel together, bound by the vow. Then quietly but savagely they rise. Othello clasps Iago's hand.)*

Othello: I greet thy love! Within these three days let me hear thee say that Cassio's not alive.

Iago: (Agreeing) My friend is dead. Tis done at your request. But let **her** live!

Othello: (Refusing with cold curses.) Damn her, lewd minx! O, damn her! *(Taking Iago's arm, for he must plan.)* Come, go with me apart. I will withdraw to furnish me with some swift means of death for the fair devil. *(In thanks, he promotes Iago.)* Now art thou my lieutenant!

Iago: (With deep devotion) I am your own forever! *(He kneels and kisses Othello's hand. The Moor looks down at his only "friend.")*

Scene 4

(Time passes, and Desdemona and Emilia take a walk outside the castle gates. Like all Venetian ladies, Desdemona wears a mask and gloves, and Emilia carries her jeweled fan. Although Desdemona frets about her lost handkerchief, her mind is chiefly on poor Cassio's problem.)

Desdemona: Where should I lose that handkerchief, Emilia?

Emilia: (Pretending innocence) I know not, madam.

Desdemona: Believe me, I had rather have lost my purse. An but my noble Moor is true of mind, it were enough to put him to ill-thinking.

Emilia: Is he not jealous?

Desdemona: (With a light laugh) Who? He? *(She has perfect faith in him.)* I think the sun where he was born drew all such humors from him.

Emilia: (Glancing down the street) Look where he comes.

Desdemona: (Ready to do her sworn duty.) I will not leave him now till Cassio be called to him! *(Removing her mask, she curtsies gracefully to*

Othello, who stares at her, silent with rage. Puzzled, she reaches up and touches his frowning face. He does not respond.) How is it with you, my lord?

Othello: (Coldly) Well, my good lady. How do you, Desdemona?

Desdemona: Well, my good lord. *(She too becomes serious, to match his mood.)*

Othello: Give me your hand! *(Taking off her glove, she places her hand in his trustingly. He examines it with care, for a warm, sweaty hand was a sign of lust.)* This hand is moist, my lady!

Desdemona: (Looking at her young hand with a smile.) It yet hath felt no age nor known no sorrow.

Othello: Hot, hot and moist! *(As if it is a sinner's hand.)* This hand of yours requires fasting and prayer, exercise devout. For here's a young and sweating devil here that commonly rebels. *(Bitterly believing that her hand has given her secret away.)* Tis a good hand... a frank one!

Desdemona: You may, indeed, say so. For 'twas that hand that gave away my heart!

Othello: (With secret meaning) A liberal hand.

Desdemona: (Changing the subject to Cassio.) Come now, your promise!

Othello: What promise, chuck?

Desdemona: I have sent to bid Cassio come speak with you!

Othello: (Feeling his eyes fill with tears, he pretends he has caught cold.) I have a salt and sorry rheum offends me. *(There is a pause. Deliberately he starts to test her.)* Lend me thy handkerchief.

Desdemona: (Giving him one from her belt.) Here, my lord.

Othello: (Pushing it away and demanding the strawberry handkerchief.) That which I gave you!

Desdemona: (Awkwardly) I have it not about me.

Othello: Not?

Desdemona: No, indeed, my lord.

Othello: That is a fault! *(To her dismay, he tells her the handkerchief is a love-charm.)* That handkerchief did an Egyptian to my mother give. She was a charmer and could almost read the thoughts of people. She told her, while she kept it, 'twould subdue my father entirely to her love. But if she lost it or made a gift of it, my father's eye should "hunt after new fancies." She, dying, gave it me and bid me, when my fate would have me wived, to give it her. I did so! And take heed on it. Make it a darling like your precious eye. *(He warns that its loss brings a terrible fate.)* To lose it or give it away were such perdition as nothing else could match!

Desdemona: Is it possible?

Othello: Tis true! There's magic in the web of it!

Desdemona: (In despair) Then would to God that I had never seen it!

Othello: (Seizing her wrist in rage.) Ha! Wherefore?

Desdemona: Why do you speak so startingly and rash?

Othello: (Roaring) Is it lost? Is it gone? Speak!

Desdemona: Heaven bless us! *(She is completely stunned, for this is a new Othello to her.)*

Othello: Say you...?

Desdemona: (In a panic, lying) It is not lost! *(She pauses, and then in a small voice, she asks the worst.)* But what if it were?

Othello: (Tightening his grip) How?

Desdemona: I say it is not lost.

Othello: (Controlling his rage, with a last hope, he pleads earnestly.) Fetch it! Let me see it!

Desdemona: (Not completely believing his anger, which is new to her, she recollects herself and turns quite dignified, as becomes a fashionable married lady. She puts her mask over her face to appear more mature.) Why, so I can, sir. But I will not now! This is a trick to put me from my suit...Pray you, let Cassio be received again!...

Othello: Fetch me the handkerchief!

Desdemona: Come, come! You'll never meet a more sufficient man...

Othello: (Fiercely) The handkerchief!

Desdemona:...a man that all his time has founded his good fortunes on your love, shared dangers with you....

Othello: (A great roar) The handkerchief!

Desdemona: (In a pretty little temper.) In sooth, you are to blame!

Othello: Away! *(Thrusting out his arm as if he thrusts her from his heart, he walks away blindly. Desdemona lowers her mask , and the women stare after him in wonder.)*

Emilia: Is not this man jealous?

Desdemona: I ne'er saw this before! *(Deeply distressed but innocent)* Sure, there's some wonder in this handkerchief. I am most unhappy in the loss of it!

Emilia: (Covering her own guilty conscience for taking the handkerchief, she comments about men in earthy terms: that as love fades, men treat women only as objects to be used.) Tis not a year or two shows us a man. They are all but stomachs, and we all but food. They eat us hungerly, and when they are full, they belch us! *(She sees new arrivals.)* Look you, Cassio and my husband.

(Iago enters in very high spirits, for he has put the handkerchief in Cassio's room, where the young man has found it. To Cassio, he insists again that only Desdemona can help his case.)

Iago: There is no other way. Tis she must do it. And lo, the happiness!

Desdemona: (Putting aside her worries to help her friend.) How now, good Cassio? What's the news with you?

Cassio: Madam, my former suit. I would not be delayed.

Desdemona: Alas, thrice-gentle Cassio... *(She hesitates, trying to find words for Othello's bad temper)*... my lord is not my lord. I have spoken for you all my best and stood his displeasure for my free speech. *(Cassio's face falls in disappointment.)* You must awhile be patient. What I can do, I will.

Iago: (Pretending surprise) Is my lord angry?

Emilia: He went hence but now, and certainly in strange un-quietness.

Iago: Can he be angry? *(Not even in battle has he seen the great Othello lose control.)* I have seen the cannon when it hath blown his ranks into the air, and, like the Devil, from his very arm puffed his own brother! *(He starts to leave.)* I will go meet him. There's matter in it indeed if he be angry!

Desdemona: I prithee, do so! *(As Iago goes, Desdemona tries to make excuses for Othello.)* Something of State, either from Venice or here in Cyprus, hath puddled his clear spirit. Tis even so.

Emilia: Pray Heaven it be State matters, as you think, and no jealous toy concerning **you!**

Desdemona: (Innocently) Alas the day! I never gave him cause.

Emilia: But jealous souls will not be answered so. They are not ever "jealous for the cause," but "jealous for they're jealous." It is a monster begot upon itself, born on itself!

Desdemona: (Frightened) Heaven keep that monster from Othello's mind!

Emilia: Lady, Amen! *(She crosses herself.)*

Desdemona: I will go seek him! Cassio, walk here about.

Cassio: I humbly thank your ladyship!

(With an elaborate bow, he sees them leave to seek the general. But no sooner are they out of sight than Bianca, a beautiful courtesan who is having an affair with handsome Cassio, comes in search of him.)

Bianca: Save you, friend Cassio!

Cassio: How is it with you, my most fair Bianca? *(He kisses her.)* In faith, sweet love, I was coming to your house.

Bianca: And I was going to your lodging, Cassio. *(She scolds him charmingly.)* What, keep a week away? Seven days and . . . nights?

Cassio: Pardon me, Bianca! *(He kisses her again, and to change the subject, he takes out Desdemona's handkerchief, as he wants the embroidery copied.)* Sweet Bianca, take me this work out.

Bianca: (Thinking he has a new love.) O Cassio, whence came this? This is some token from a newer friend. Well, well!

Cassio: Go to, woman! You are jealous now that this is from some mistress, some remembrance. No, in

good troth, Bianca! *(He smiles, and she is dazzled but unconvinced.)*

Bianca: Why, whose is it?

Cassio: I know not. I found it in my chamber. I like the work well. I would have it copied. Take it and do it, and leave me for this time.

Bianca: Leave you? Wherefore? *(She takes the handkerchief.)*

Cassio: I do attend here on the general.

Bianca: (With a flirtatious pout) You do not love me! *(He kisses her pretty mouth with passion, and she coaxes him to go towards home with her.)* I pray you, bring me on the way a little, and say if I shall see you soon at night.

Cassio: (With an uneasy look about, to see if Othello is coming back.) Tis but a little way that I can bring you. I'll see you soon.

Bianca: (Comfortably taking his arm.) Tis very good! *(They stroll off, smiling and kissing.)*

ACT IV

Scene 1

(The same scene continues, as Iago returns with Othello, continuing to poison the Moor's shaken mind with invented details of his wife's adultery. Consumed with jealousy, Othello now believes everything his "honest" friend says.)

Iago: Will you think so?

Othello: Think so, Iago?

Iago: What, to kiss in private?

Othello: An unauthorized kiss?

Iago: (Taunting him further) Or to be naked with her friend in bed an hour or more, not meaning any harm?

Othello: (Thunderstruck) Naked in bed, Iago, and not mean harm? It is hypocrisy against the Devil!

Iago: (Shrugging off such minor sins.) So they do nothing . . . tis a venial slip. But if I give my wife a handkerchief. . . .

Othello: (He stops and looks Iago directly in the face.) What then?

Iago: (Not returning the glance) Why, then tis hers, my lord. And being hers, she may, I think, bestow it on any man.

Othello: She is protectress of her honor too. May she give that?

Iago: (Shrugging again at virtue, which, invisible, can be false.) Her honor is an essence that's not seen. They "have it" very oft that have it not. But for the handkerchief....

Othello: By Heaven, I would most gladly have forgot it. Thou saidst...he had my handkerchief!

Iago: Ay, what of that?

Othello: (Slowly) That's...not...so...good...now.

Iago: What if I had said I had seen him do you wrong? Or heard him say....

Othello: (Almost frightened to ask) What hath he said?

Iago: Faith, that he did...*(Reluctantly)*...I know not what he did.

Othello: (Stammering with horror) What? What?

Iago: Lie...

Othello: With her?

Iago: "With" her..."on" her—what you will.

Othello: Lie with her? Lie on her? *(He rages in broken speech.)* Lie with her! That's fulsome...handkerchief...confessions...handkerchief...to confess and be hanged for his labor...I tremble at it!

(He falls to the ground in a fit of epilepsy. Iago, coldly smiling, hovers over Othello's unconscious body like an evil spirit, gloating.)

Iago: Work on, my medicine, work! Thus fools are caught! *(Seeing Cassio approach, he kneels to try to revive Othello.)* What, ho! My lord! My lord, I say! Othello! *(Turning to Cassio, who has rushed to kneel also at his general's side.)* How now, Cassio?

Cassio: What's the matter?

Iago: My lord is fallen into an epilepsy. This is his second fit. He had one yesterday.

Cassio: Rub him about the temples!

Iago: (Othello moves and groans.) Look, he stirs. Do you withdraw yourself a little while. He will recover straight. When he is gone, I would speak with you. *(Cassio nods and leaves, as Othello comes to his senses. Dazed, he props himself up on one elbow. Iago tends him gently.)* How is it, general? Have you not hurt your head?

Othello: (Taking the remark to refer to the horns of a betrayed husband.) Dost thou mock me?

Iago: I mock you? No, by Heaven. Bear your fortune like a man!

Othello: A horned man's a monster and a beast.

Iago: (Emphasizing the corruption of town life.) There's many a beast then in a populous city.

(He helps the Moor rise and assists him to an archway nearby, where Othello can hide and watch what goes on.) Good sir, stand you awhile apart. Whilst you were here, o'erwhelmed with your grief—a passion most unfitting such a

man—Cassio came hither. I shifted him away and bade him return and here speak with me, the which he promised.

I will make him tell the tale anew: where, how, how oft, how long ago and when he hath and is again to "cope" your wife. *(As Othello puts his hand on his sword-hilt.)* Marry, patience!

(Othello hides behind the pillar, able to see but too far away to hear any conversation. Iago, chuckling, thinks aloud to himself.)

Now will I question Cassio of Bianca. It is a creature that dotes on Cassio. He, when he hears of her, cannot refrain from the excess of laughter. Here he comes! *(When the handsome young officer enters, Iago adds to himself.)* As he shall smile, Othello shall go mad! *(Loudly)* How do you now, lieutenant?

Cassio: The worser. *(He bites his lip with misery at hearing his former title.)*

Iago: Now, if this suit lay in Bianca's power, how quickly should you speed!

Cassio: *(Laughing at the thought of the love-sick courtesan.)* Alas, poor caitiff!

Othello: *(Watching, yet unable to hear anything, he speaks to himself.)* Look how he laughs already!

Iago: *(With easy coarseness)* I never knew a woman love man so!

Cassio: *(Flattered, laughing more)* Alas, poor rogue. I think, in faith, she loves me!

Othello: (Misunderstanding completely, he thinks Cassio's laughter is aimed at himself, the wronged husband.) So, so, so, so . . . they laugh that win!

Iago: (Keeping the joke going) Faith, the cry goes that you shall marry her!

Cassio: She is persuaded I will marry her out of her own love, not out of my promise. *(As he tells Iago of Bianca's love-sickness, Iago secretly gestures for Othello to move closer to hear.)*

Othello: Iago beckons me. Now he begins the story.

(As Othello listens, he thinks the "she" of the story is Desdemona, not foolish Bianca.)

Cassio: She was here even now. She haunts me in every place! I was the other day talking on the sea bank with certain Venetians, and thither comes the bauble and falls me thus about my neck . . . *(He hangs on Iago's neck to illustrate. Iago laughs like a good sport, encouraging him.)*

Othello: . . . crying, "O dear Cassio!" as it were!

Cassio: . . . so hangs, and lolls and weeps upon me, so hales and pulls me! Ha, ha, ha! *(He imitates her inviting little tugs.)*

Othello: (To himself) Now he tells how she plucked him to my chamber. *(He turns away, unwilling to listen further.)*

Iago: (Looking off and exclaiming in surprise.) Look where she comes!

Cassio: (Greeting his mistress with some irritation as she enters, angry.) What do you mean by this

Othello: By Heaven, that should be my handkerchief!

haunting of me? *(Othello returns to hear more, edging even closer.)*

Bianca: Let the Devil and his dam haunt you! *(Jealously)* What did you mean by that same handkerchief you gave me even now? I was a fine fool to take it. I must "take out the work"? A likely piece of work—that you should find it in your chamber and not know who left it there! *(She swears he has another mistress.)* This is some minx's token. There! *(She throws down the strawberry handkerchief in scorn.)*

Cassio: How now, my sweet Bianca? How now? How now? *(He picks up the handkerchief, laughs, and waves it about with graceful gestures. Othello can see easily what Cassio holds.)*

Othello: By Heaven, that should be my handkerchief!

Bianca: (To Cassio, sharply) An you'll come to supper tonight, you may. *(But if he does not come, he can wait for an invitation.)* An you will not, come when you are next prepared for! *(In a fit of anger, she leaves.)*

Iago: (Pushing Cassio) After her, after her!

Cassio: Faith, I must. *(He does not want to lose such a lively wench.)*

Iago: Will you sup there?

Cassio: Faith, I intend so.

Iago: Well, I may chance to see you, for I would speak with you. *(Cassio runs after Bianca, laughing and waving the handkerchief.)*

Othello: (Coming forward, blood-thirsty) How shall I murder him, Iago?

Iago: (Seriously) Did you perceive how he laughed at his vice?

Othello: O Iago!

Iago: And did you see the handkerchief?

Othello: (Asking without hope) Was that mine?

Iago: Yours, by this hand! And to see how he prizes the foolish woman, your wife! She gave it him, and he hath given it his whore.

Othello: (He wants a long torture session.) I would have him nine years a-killing! *(With a moan, he thinks of his lovely high-born bride.)* A fine woman, a fair woman, a sweet woman.

Iago: Nay, you must forget that!

Othello: Ay, let her rot and perish and be damned tonight, for she shall not live. No, my heart is turned to stone. *(He beats his chest.)* I strike it and it hurts my hand. *(Yet the thought of Desdemona makes him realize her many good qualities.)* O, the world hath not a sweeter creature! She might lie by an emperor's side and command him tasks.

Iago: Nay, that's not your way! *(He frowns that his general might change his mind and pardon Desdemona.)*

Othello: Hang her! I do but say what she is. *(Again her many Venetian charms overwhelm him.)* So delicate with her needle. An admirable musician. O, she will sing the savageness out of a bear! Of so high and plenteous wit and invention . . .

Iago: She's the worse for all this!

Othello: Nay, that's certain. *(Overcome by such goodness gone wrong.)* But yet the pity of it, Iago! O Iago, the pity of it, Iago!

Iago: O, tis foul in her!

Othello: With mine officer!

Iago: That's fouler!

Othello: Get me some poison, Iago, this night! *(He will not try to argue with her, for fear she will change his mind.)* I'll not expostulate with her, lest her body and beauty unprovide my mind again. *(With haste, for tonight she must die.)* This night, Iago!

Iago: Do it not with poison. *(A better idea)* Strangle her in her bed, even the bed she hath contaminated.

Othello: Good, good! The justice of it pleases. Very good!

Iago: And for Cassio, let me be his undertaker! *(With a savage chuckle)* You shall hear more by midnight.

Othello: Excellent good! *(A trumpet in the distance sounds a welcome to new arrivals.)* What trumpet is that same?

Iago: Something from Venice, sure.

(As they watch, a procession comes from the harbor. In it are Desdemona and her attendants. They accompany a handsome courtier from Venice, Lodovico, who is Desdemona's cousin.)

Tis Lodovico, come from the Duke. And, see, your wife is with him.

Lodovico: (With a bow and look of great admiration for Othello.) Save you, worthy general!

Othello: (Returning the greeting, but with a serious face.) With all my heart, sir.

Lodovico: The Duke and Senators of Venice greet you. *(He hands Othello a parchment scroll.)*

Othello: I kiss the instrument of their pleasures. *(Respectfully he presses his lips to the wax seal before breaking open the letter.)*

Desdemona: (Happy to hear from home.) And what's the news, good Cousin Lodovico?

Iago: (Greeting the envoy with a clumsy bow.) I am very glad to see you, Signior. Welcome to Cyprus!

Lodovico: I thank you. *(Casually he turns from Iago, as a lower-class person, and looks about for a friend of his.)* How does Lieutenant Cassio?

Iago: (Shortly) Lives, sir.

Desdemona: Cousin, there's fallen between him and my lord an unkind breach. *(Happily)* But you shall make all well!

Othello: (Raising his head from the letter with a frown.) Are you sure of that?

Desdemona: (Startled) My lord?

Othello: (Reading aloud) "This fail you not to do, as you will...."

Lodovico: (To Desdemona) He did not call. He's busy in the paper. *(On a personal note)* Is there division twixt my lord and Cassio?

Desdemona: A most unhappy one. *(Explaining innocently about her friend.)* I would do much to atone them, for the love I bear to Cassio.

Othello: (Savagely) Fire and brimstone!

Desdemona: (Startled again) My lord?

Lodovico: May be the letter moved him. *(He knows the contents.)* For, as I think, they do command him home, deputing Cassio in his government.

Desdemona: (Happy that Cassio will have a good new position as governor of Cyprus.) Trust me, I am glad on it!

Othello: Indeed? *(The more she speaks, the more he misunderstands her, and his anger wells up to fury.)*

Desdemona: (Confused) Why, sweet Othello....

Othello: Devil! *(Raising his hand, he strikes her hard across the face.)*

Desdemona: I have not deserved this! *(Her hand goes to her cheek, and tears well in her eyes. All the courtiers murmur in astonishment.)*

Lodovico: My lord, this would not be believed in Venice, though I should swear I saw it! Tis very much! *(Trying to make peace)* Make her amends. She weeps!

Othello: Devil!

Othello: (Pointing away as he bellows at her.) O Devil, Devil! Out of my sight!

Desdemona: I will not stay to offend you! *(She starts to leave, weak with shock.)*

Lodovico: Truly, an obedient lady. *(To Othello, whom he has so admired.)* I do beseech your lordship, call her back!

Othello: (Stopping her with a roar of command.) Mistress!

Desdemona: (Half-turning) My lord?

Othello: (To Lodovico) What would you with her, sir?

Lodovico: (Confused) Who? I, my lord?

Othello: Ay! You did wish that I would make her turn. *(In a mocking tone, sure that Desdemona can pretend any false effect.)* Sir, she can turn and turn and yet go on and turn again. And she can weep, sir, weep! And she's obedient, as you say, obedient, very obedient. *(In a roar to Desdemona.)* Proceed you in your tears!

(As if obeying, she bursts into sobs. Othello waves the paper at Lodovico.) Concerning this, sir...*(To his wife, sarcastically)* O well-painted passion! *(To Lodovico again)*...I am commanded home. *(To Desdemona)* Get you away! I'll send for you anon. *(To Lodovico with fury)* Sir, I obey the mandate and will return to Venice! *(To Desdemona)* Hence, avaunt!

(She leaves, bitterly crying. The Moor clenches his hand on his gold chain-of-office and whirls to Lodovico again.) Cassio shall have my place!

And, sir, tonight I do entreat that we may sup together. You are welcome, sir, to Cyprus! *(With a short bow, he sweeps off in a trembling rage.)* Goats and monkeys!

Lodovico: (Looking after Othello with astonishment to find him so changed from his usual calm self.) Is this the noble Moor whom our full Senate call all-in-all sufficient? Is this the nature whom passion could not shake?

Iago: He is much changed.

Lodovico: (Tapping his head to indicate insanity.) Are his wits safe? Is he not light of brain?

Iago: (Not answering directly) He's . . . that he is.

Lodovico: (Unable to believe his own eyes.) What, strike his wife?

Iago: Alas, alas! *(He puts up his hand to stop further questions.)* It is not honesty in me to speak what I have seen and know. *(Lodovico nods, respecting the rough fellow's loyalty to his general.)* You shall observe him. Do but go after, and mark how he continues! *(With a wide gesture, he motions Lodovico to see more.)*

Lodovico: I am sorry that I am deceived in him! *(Together they exit thoughtfully.)*

Scene 2

(In a chamber of the Citadel, Othello interrogates Emilia about her mistress and Cassio. He is still

enraged, distrusting the woman's simple answers, and his short questions whip across the air at break-neck pace.)

Othello: You have seen nothing then?

Emilia: Nor ever heard, nor ever did suspect.

Othello: Yes, you have seen Cassio and she together!

Emilia: (Protesting) But then I saw no harm. *(Firmly)* And then I heard each syllable between them!

Othello: What, did they never whisper?

Emilia: Never, my lord.

Othello: Nor send you out of the way?

Emilia: Never!

Othello: To fetch her fan, her gloves, her mask, nor nothing?

Emilia: Never, my lord!

Othello: Bid her come hither. Go! *(Emilia leaves to fetch Desdemona, but her plain face is deeply worried. Othello looks after the woman with deep suspicion.)* She says enough. *(Nevertheless, any brothel keeper would say the same.)* Yet she's a simple bawd that cannot say as much. *(Thinking of his wife's sophisticated cleverness.)* This is a subtle whore. She'll kneel and pray. I have seen her do it. *(Emilia returns with Desdemona, who looks at Othello timidly.)*

Desdemona: My lord, what is your will?

Othello: (Roughly, as if he is a soldier like Iago.) Pray, chuck, come hither!

Desdemona: (Advancing to him) What is your pleasure?

Othello: (Pointing for her to kneel at his feet.) Let me see your eyes. Look in my face!

Desdemona: (Kneeling) What horrible fancy's this?

Othello: (To Emilia, as if she is the madam of a brothel.) Mistress, leave procreants alone and shut the door. Cough or cry, "Hem!" if anybody come. *(Emilia is to work her trade as procuress.)* Your mystery, your mystery! Nay, dispatch! *(Emilia leaves at his angry voice.)*

Desdemona: Upon my knees, what doth your speech import? I understand a fury in your words, but not the words.

Othello: (Looking deep into her eyes, trying to read her soul.) Why, what art thou?

Desdemona: Your wife, my lord. Your true and loyal wife!

Othello: Come, swear it! Swear thou art honest.

Desdemona: (Crossing herself) Heaven doth truly know it.

Othello: (Spitting the words straight into her face.) Heaven truly knows that thou art false as Hell!

Desdemona: (Thunderstruck) To whom, my lord? With whom? How am I false?

Othello: (Pushing her aside and walking off.) Ah, Desdemona! Away! Away! Away! *(He sobs in desolation.)*

Desdemona: Alas the heavy day! *(With pity for him)* Why do you weep? Am I the motive of these tears, my lord? *(It occurs to her that his anger is caused by her father's influence in ordering Othello back to Venice.)* If haply you my father do suspect an instrument of this your calling back, lay not your blame on me. *(She will join her husband against her father.)* If you have lost him, why, I have lost him too!

Othello: (In absolute dismay, for if God had sent him sickness, poverty or imprisonment, he should have been able to endure it.) Had it pleased Heaven to try me with affliction, had they rained all kinds of sores and shames on my bare head, steeped me in poverty to the very lips, given to captivity me and my utmost hopes—I should have found in some place of my soul a drop of patience.

(But he finds his innermost heart is thrown away or kept a slimy toad's nest, where even saintly Patience loses color.) But there where I have garnered up my heart, where either I must live or bear no life, the fountain from the which my current runs or else dries up—to be discarded thence, or keep it as a cistern for foul toads to knot and gender in—turn thy complexion there, Patience, thou young and rose-lipped cherubin! Ay, there, look grim as Hell!

Desdemona: (Not understanding him at all.) I hope my noble lord esteems me honest.

Othello: (With sarcasm) O, ay, as summer flies are. *(He takes her beautiful face between his hands and wishes she were dead.)* O thou weed, who art so lovely fair and smellst so sweet that the sense aches at thee, would thou hadst ne'er been born!

Desdemona: Alas, what ignorant sin have I committed?

Othello: (Passing his fingers over her cheeks.) Was this fair paper, this most goodly book, made to write "Whore" upon? *(He traces the letters of the word upon her forehead as he repeats her question.)* What, "committed?" "Committed?" "What committed?" *(All Nature shrinks away from her great guilt.)* Heaven stops the nose at it. And the moon winks. The bawdy wind that kisses all it meets is hushed within the hollow mine of earth and will not hear it. "What committed?" Impudent strumpet! *(He sobs again.)*

Desdemona: (In desperation) By Heaven, you do me wrong!

Othello: Are not you a strumpet?

Desdemona: No, as I am a Christian!

Othello: (Not believing a word) What, not a whore?

Desdemona: No, as I shall be saved!

Othello: Is it possible?

Desdemona: (A prayer for help, which Othello takes as a confession.) O Heaven forgive us!

Othello: (Apologizing with heavy scorn) I cry you mercy then. I took you for that cunning whore of Venice that married with Othello. *(Calling to Emilia, as if to the madam of the house.)* You, mistress, that keep the Gate of Hell! *(Emilia enters, frowning.)* You, you ay, you! We have done our course. There's money for your pains! *(Throws some coins at her feet as if in payment.)* I pray you turn the key. *(He leaves, burying his face in his hands.)*

Emilia: (Picking up the coins with wonder.) Alas, what does this gentleman conceive? *(Turning to Desdemona, who lies half-fainting on the floor.)* How do you, madam? How do you, my good lady?

Desdemona: Faith, half-asleep.

Emilia: Good madam, what's the matter with my lord? *(She helps her to a stool.)*

Desdemona: With who? *(She puts her hand to her head, bewildered.)*

Emilia: Why, with my lord, madam.

Desdemona: Who is thy lord?

Emilia: (Convinced the world has gone mad.) He that is yours, sweet lady! *(She jerks her thumb after Othello. Desdemona shakes her head sadly.)*

Desdemona: I have none. Do not talk to me, Emilia. I cannot weep, nor answer have I none. *(With a sudden thought)* Prithee, tonight lay on my bed my wedding sheets, remember, and call thy husband hither.

Emilia: (Scratching her head) Here's a change indeed! *(Shrugging, she leaves to change the bed-linen, but at the door she meets Iago.)*

Desdemona: (To herself, trying to agree with Othello that she deserves punishment, somehow.) Tis meet I should be used so, very meet.

Iago: (Crossing to her sympathetically) What is your pleasure, madam? How is it with you?

Desdemona: I cannot tell.

Emilia: (Angry at the unfairness of it all.) Alas, Iago, my lord hath so be-whored her, thrown heavy terms upon her, as true hearts cannot bear.

Desdemona: (Faintly) Am I that name, Iago?

Iago: What name, fair lady?

Desdemona: (She cannot force herself to say the filthy word, so she points to Emilia.) Such as she said my lord did say I was.

Emilia: (With no delicacy at all.) He called her, "Whore!"

Iago: (Pretending to be shocked) Why did he so?

Desdemona: I do not know. I am sure I am none such. *(Simply, she begins to cry.)*

Iago: Do not weep. Do not weep! *(Pretending to weep himself)* Alas the day!

Emilia: (Furious at Othello, for whom Desdemona has sacrificed everything.) Hath she forsook so many noble matches, her father and her country, and her friends, to be called, "Whore"? Would it not make one weep?

Iago: How comes this trick upon him?

Desdemona: (Helplessly) Nay, Heaven doth know.

Emilia: (With an inspired thought that some schemer has done this to get Othello's friendship and promotion.) I will be hanged if some eternal villain, some busy and insinuating rogue, some cogging, cozening slave, to get some office, have not devised this slander! I'll be hanged else!

Iago: (Alarmed, for she has unconsciously spoken the truth, he contradicts her.) Fie, there is no such man. It is impossible!

Desdemona: If any such there be, Heaven pardon him.

Emilia: (She would rather see the liar hanged.) A halter pardon him! And Hell gnaw his bones! *(Returning to the false charges.)* Why should he call her, "Whore"? *(She knows there is no lover.)* Who keeps her company? What place? What time?

Iago: (Trying to quiet her loud voice.) Speak within door!

Emilia: O, fie upon them! *(She remarks that the same type of villain said she was sleeping with Othello.)* Some such squire he was that turned your wit and made you to suspect me with the Moor!

Iago: You are a fool. Go to!

Desdemona: O good Iago, what shall I do to win my lord again? *(Desperate for help)* Good friend, go to him, for, by this light of Heaven, I know not how I lost him. Here I kneel! *(She gets upon her knees—the naive young wife, ready to accept*

Othello's cruelty to death but never to stop loving him.) Unkindness may do much, and his unkindness may defeat my life but never taint my love.

I cannot say, "Whore." *(She wipes her mouth with the back of her hand.)* To do the act, not the world could make me!

Iago: I pray you, be content. *(Blaming the troubles of government.)* The business of the State does him offense, and he does chide with you.

Desdemona: (Doubtfully) If 'twere no other...

Iago: Tis but so, I warrant! *(Trumpets sound the call to the formal dinner for Lodovico and the newly arrived Venetians.)* Hark how these instruments summon to supper. Go in and weep not. All things shall be well! *(Emilia helps Desdemona leave to dress for the feast. Iago looks after them and laughs in relief. His secret villainy has not been discovered. But in comes Roderigo, looking sulky. Iago greets him with high good humor, for lately he has cheated Roderigo out of a pocketful of jewels, which he pretended to give Desdemona.)* How now, Roderigo?

Roderigo: I do not find that thou dealst justly with me!

Iago: What?

Roderigo: (He drags out his empty purse.) I have wasted myself out of my means. *(His gems would have seduced a nun, but not Desdemona.)* The jewels you have had from me to deliver Desdemona would half have corrupted a votarist. You have told me she hath received them and returned me expectations. But I find none!

Iago: Well, go to. Very well. *(He dismisses the problem easily.)*

Roderigo: "Very well"? "Go to"? *(In a temper)* I cannot "go to," man! Nor tis not "very well"! Nay, I think it is scurvy! I will make myself known to Desdemona. If she will return me my jewels, I will give over my suit and repent. *(He half-draws his sword to threaten Iago with a duel.)* If not, assure yourself I will "seek satisfaction" of you!

Iago: (Pretending to be amazed at Roderigo's spirit.) Why, now I see there's mettle in thee! Give me thy hand, Roderigo! *(He pumps his arm and slaps him on the back. Roderigo smiles weakly at this demonstration of popularity.)* Yet I protest I have dealt most directly in thy affair!

Roderigo: It hath not appeared.

Iago: I grant indeed it hath not appeared, and your suspicion is not without wit and judgment. *(Roderigo tries to look intelligent to fit the compliment, as Iago continues his flattery and promises.)* But, Roderigo, if thou hast purpose, courage, and valor—this night show it! If thou the next night following "enjoy" not Desdemona, take me from this world with treachery! *(He draws his own knife and offers it, with his life, to Roderigo.)*

Roderigo: (Wanting to know Iago's plan.) Well, what is it?

Iago: Sir, there is especial commission come from Venice to depute Cassio in Othello's place.

Roderigo: Is that true? *(Iago nods.)* Why, then Othello and Desdemona return again to Venice.

Iago: O no, he goes into Mauritania and takes away with him the fair Desdemona...*(Roderigo's face falls.)*...unless...*(Roderigo's face brightens.)* ...his abode be lingered here by some accident ...as the removing of Cassio.

Roderigo: How do you mean, "removing" of him?

Iago: Why, knocking out his brains.

Roderigo: And that you would have me to do?

Iago: Ay, if you dare! *(Pointing out the castle window towards Bianca's house, where Cassio dines.)* He sups tonight with a harlotry, and thither will I go to him. *(He plans an ambush on Cassio's way home.)* If you will watch his going thence, which I will fashion to fall out between twelve and one, he shall fall between us. *(Grinning, he stabs the air with his dagger.)* Come, stand not amazed, but go along with me!

Roderigo: *(Eagerly)* I will hear further reason for this!

Iago: And you shall be satisfied! *(Like comrades, they leave, Iago's arm about Roderigo.)*

Scene 3

(At the door of Desdemona's bedchamber, Othello and his guest Lodovico pause while the Moor gives

his wife instructions, and Lodovico bids his fair cousin good-night. Desdemona stands obediently. In the background, Emilia places Desdemona's night-robe ready and turns down the bed.)

Lodovico: Madam, good night. I humbly thank your ladyship. *(He bows.)*

Desdemona: (With a curtsey) Your honor is most welcome.

Othello: O, Desdemona...

Desdemona: (In a humble voice) My lord?

Othello:...get you to bed on the instant. I will be returned forthwith. *(Gesturing towards Emilia)* Dismiss your attendant there. Look it be done. *(His orders are short but not angry.)*

Desdemona: I will, my lord. *(Othello leaves with Lodovico, who looks back at his young cousin with grave worry.)*

Emilia: How goes it now? *(She comes forward with a doubtful air.)* He looks gentler than he did.

Desdemona: He says he will return. He hath commanded me to go to bed and bade me to dismiss you.

Emilia: (Her lips set firmly in disapproval.) I would you had never seen him!

Desdemona: So would not I. *(She loves him even when he scolds.)* My love doth so approve him that even his stubbornness, his checks, his frowns —prithee, un-pin me!—have grace and favor in them! *(Emilia unfastens her gown at the back and slips it off her, so Desdemona stands in her petticoat and elaborate sleeves.)*

Emilia: I have laid those sheets you bade me on the bed. *(She smiles with real affection at her young mistress.)*

Desdemona: (With a shrug) All's one. *(A death-thought comes to her, and she crosses herself.)* Good faith, how foolish are our minds! *(To Emilia, sadly, wanting to be buried in her wedding linen.)* If I do die before thee, prithee shroud me in one of those same sheets.

Emilia: (Soothingly) Come, come, you talk.

Desdemona: (As she starts to brush her hair, she thinks of a sad love story in the past.) My mother had a maid called Barbara. She was in love. And he she loved proved mad, and did forsake her. She had a song of "Willow." An old thing 'twas, but it expressed her fortune, and she died singing it. That song tonight will not go from my mind. *(She lets her head fall sadly.)* I have much to do but to go hang my head all at one side and sing it like poor Barbara.

Emilia: Shall I go fetch your nightgown?

Desdemona: No, un-pin me here. *(Emilia removes the separate sleeves, while Desdemona talks of her attractive cousin.)* This Lodovico is a proper man.

Emilia: A very handsome man! *(She gives a cheerful whistle of approval.)*

Desdemona: He speaks well.

Emilia: (Laughing at his effect on women.) I know a lady in Venice would have walked barefoot to Palestine for a touch of his nether lip!

Desdemona: (Sings softly as she slips out of her embroidered petticoat and stands in her simple under-smock.)

The poor soul sat sighing by a sycamore tree,
Sing all a green willow.
Her hand on her bosom, her head on her knee,

Sing willow, willow, willow.
The fresh streams ran by her and murmured her moans.

Sing willow, willow, willow.
Her salt tears fell from her and softened the stones . . .

(To Emilia, giving her the petticoat and some jewels.) Lay by these.

Sing willow, willow, willow . . . .

(To Emilia, to hurry) Prithee, hie thee! He'll come anon!

Sing all a green willow must be my garland.
Let nobody blame him, his scorn I approve . . . .

(She breaks off singing.) Nay, that's not next. *(Listening)* Hark! Who is it that knocks?

Emilia: It is the wind. *(She helps the girl put on her long white night-robe over her smock, and arranges the rich border of Venetian lace.)*

Desdemona: (Singing)

I called my love "false love," but what said he then?

Sing willow, willow, willow.
"If I court more women, you'll couch with more men . . . ."

(To Emilia) So, get thee gone. Good night. *(She rubs her eyes like a child.)* Mine eyes do itch. *(Wondering if it foretells she will cry soon.)* Doth that bode weeping?

Emilia: (With a shrug of unconcern.) Tis neither here nor there.

Desdemona: I have heard it said so. *(With a sigh)* O, these men, these men! *(Suddenly wanting to know about women who commit adultery.)* Dost thou think, Emilia, that there be women do abuse their husbands in such gross kind?

Emilia: (Matter-of-factly, as she has seen much of the world.) There be some such, no question.

Desdemona: (Curious) Wouldst thou do such a deed for all the world?

Emilia: Why, would not you?

Desdemona: (Shyly) No, by this heavenly light!

Emilia: Nor I neither by this heavenly light. *(She chuckles and winks broadly.)* I might do it as well in the dark!

Desdemona: (Shocked that her friend might even think of such an act.) Wouldst thou do such a deed for all the world?

Emilia: *(Thinking how much gold the world is worth.)* The world's a huge thing. It is a great price for a small vice!

Desdemona: In troth, I think thou wouldst not!

Emilia: In troth, I think I should! *(And then she would take it all back later.)* And un-do it when I had done. *(She would not cheat on her husband for small gifts.)* Marry, I would not do such a thing for a joint-ring, nor for measures of lawn, nor for gowns, petticoats nor caps, nor any petty exhibition. *(She laughs aloud, running her hands through imaginary piles of gold and thinking of her cheated husband as rich as a king.)* But for the whole world? Why, who would not make her husband a "cuckold" to make him a monarch? *(She would risk a little punishment.)* I should venture Purgatory for it!

Desdemona: *(Unable to agree)* I do not think there is any such woman!

Emilia: Yes, a dozen. *(She pauses and puts the blame squarely on the men.)* But I do think it is their husbands' faults if wives do fall. *(Either they do not make love to them often enough, or else they are cruel.)* Say that they slack their "duties," or else break out in peevish jealousies, or say they strike us. *(When wives are hurt, they can get even.)* Why, we have galls, yet have we some revenge!

(Women are the same as men.) Let husbands know their wives have sense like them. They see and smell and have their palates both for sweet and

sour, as husbands have. *(When husbands cheat on wives, the men enjoy it because of desires and weaknesses.)* What is it that they do when they change us for others?...Is it sport? I think it is...And doth affection breed it? I think it doth...Is it frailty that thus errs? It is so too. *(So women have the same desires, pleasures and weaknesses.)* And have not we affections? ...desires for sport?...and frailty?... as men have?

(With a warning that husbands should be faithful to their wives, or the wives will copy their bad examples.) Then let them use us well! Else, let them know the "ills" we do, their "ills" instruct us so!

Desdemona: (Shaking her head, she cannot agree at all.) Good night. Good night. *(Emilia, still chuckling, pulls the bed curtains half-closed and leaves. Desdemona tries to sleep, but she turns over and weeps instead.)*

ACT V

Scene 1

(In a street at midnight, Iago leads the foolish Roderigo to a spot where a projecting side of a shop makes a good hiding place. Here they will ambush Cassio as he returns from supper at Bianca's house.)

Iago: Here, stand behind this bulk. Straight will he come. *(Pulling Roderigo's sword out of its sheath.)* Wear thy good rapier bare. Quick, quick! Fear nothing. I'll be at thy elbow.

Roderigo: (To himself, as he looks after Iago.) I have no great devotion to the deed, and yet he hath given me satisfying reasons. *(He shrugs, for murder is not important.)* Tis but a man gone. Forth, my sword! *(He lunges for practice.)* He dies!

Iago: (To himself, watching Roderigo scornfully, as he does not care who kills whom.) Now, whether he kill Cassio or Cassio him, or each do kill the other, every way makes my gain! *(He certainly does not want the swindled Roderigo to survive.)* Live Roderigo, he calls me to a restitution large of gold and jewels that I bobbed from him as gifts to Desdemona. It must not be!

(And Cassio's manner makes Iago look bad.) If Cassio do remain, he hath a daily beauty in his life that makes me ugly. *(Also Othello may check Iago's lies with Cassio.)* And besides, the Moor may unfold me to him. There stand I in much

peril! No, he must die! *(Suddenly alert)* But so, I hear him coming. *(Cassio enters, humming a tune as he strolls back to his inn.)*

Roderigo: Tis he! *(He thrusts his sword at Cassio.)* Villain, thou diest!

Cassio: (Proud of his sword-proof coat.) That thrust had been mine enemy indeed but that my coat is better than thou knowst. *(He draws his weapon.)* I will make proof of thine!

(With clash and clatter, he fights with Roderigo up and down the dark street. At last Roderigo falls, seriously wounded. From the shadows, Iago reaches out, quickly slashes Cassio across the back of the leg, and runs away.)

Roderigo: O, I am slain!

Cassio: (Holding his badly gashed leg.) I am maimed forever! *(Calling out in the night.)* Help, ho! Murder! Murder! *(He falls to the ground.)*

(To one side, Othello comes in silently, listening to Cassio's cries. He does not move to help his former officer.)

Othello: (Whispering to himself) The voice of Cassio! Iago keeps his word.

Cassio: (Shouting) O help, ho! Light! A surgeon!

Othello: Tis he! O brave Iago, honest and just, thou teachest me. *(He too will kill as planned, and he calls softly to Desdemona as if she were there.)* Minion, your dear lies dead. Strumpet, I come. *(Stealthily as a wild animal he glides away.)*

(For a moment all is still, except for the cries of the wounded. Then a torch appears at the door of a house. Lodovico and another Venetian—Old Gratiano, who is Brabantio's brother and Desdemona's uncle—look out into the dark.)

Cassio: What, ho? No watch? Murder! Murder!

Gratiano: (Alarmed but cautious) Tis some mischance! The cry is very direful.

Roderigo: O wretched villain!

Lodovico: Two or three groan! It is a heavy night. *(Alarmed that it may be a trap, he does not dare leave the doorway.)* These may be counterfeits. Let's think it unsafe to come in to the cry without more help.

Roderigo: (A thin wail) Nobody come? Then shall I bleed to death!

Lodovico: Hark!

(Iago enters with a torch, his jacket off as if he has been roused from sleep in his shirt and hose. He wears a dagger.)

Gratiano: Here's one comes in his shirt, with light and weapons.

Iago: (Peering up and down the street.) Who's there? Whose noise is this that cries on murder?

Cassio: (With a weak shout) Here, here! For Heaven's sake, help me! *(Cautiously Iago approaches the wounded.)*

Gratiano: (As he catches sight of Iago's face in the torchlight.) This is Othello's ancient, as I take it.

Iago: What are you here that cry so grievously? *(His light falls on Cassio.)*

Cassio: Iago? O, I am spoiled, undone by villains. *(Feebly)* Give me some help!

Iago: (As if horrified) O me, lieutenant! What villains have done this?

Cassio: (With a wave in Roderigo's direction.) I think that one of them is here about and cannot make away.

Iago: O treacherous villains! *(Calling to Lodovico and Old Gratiano, still at the doorway.)* What are you there? Come in, and give some help!

Roderigo: (A faint cry) O, help me here!

Cassio: (To Iago) That's one of them!

Iago: (Leaving his torch with Cassio, he rushes to Roderigo, who puts out his hand in friendship. But Iago draws his dagger.) O murderous slave! O villain! *(In the dark, unseen by the others, he stabs Roderigo neatly.)*

Roderigo: (A last whimper) O damned Iago. O inhuman dog! *(He dies.)*

Iago: Kill men in the dark? *(He secretly wipes his blade clean on Roderigo's clothes and then rises, pretending to hunt further for Cassio's attackers.)* Where be these bloody thieves? How silent is this town! *(He walks around innocently, coming across Lodovico and Old Gratiano still in the doorway.)* Signior Lodovico?

Lodovico: He, sir.

Iago: (With a bow) I cry your mercy. *(Pointing)* Here's Cassio hurt by villains!

Gratiano: Cassio? *(They go with Iago to help.)*

Iago: (Kneeling by the young officer with sympathy.) How is it, brother?

Cassio: My leg is cut in two!

Iago: Marry, Heaven forbid! *(To the others)* Light, gentlemen! *(Lodovico holds the torch so Iago can give delayed help.)* I'll bind it with my shirt. *(He rips the cloth to bandage Cassio's leg.)*

Bianca: (Entering from down the street, aroused by the noise.) What is the matter, ho? Who is it that cried?

Iago: (Mocking her) "Who is it that cried?"

Bianca: (At the sight of the victim.) O my dear Cassio! My sweet Cassio! O Cassio, Cassio, Cassio!

Iago: (Pushing her away with scorn.) O notable strumpet! *(To his supposed friend)* Cassio, may you suspect who they should be that have thus mangled you? *(He binds his leg roughly.)*

Cassio: No. *(He grits his teeth with the pain.)*

Iago: (Rudely to Bianca) Lend me a garter. *(When she raises her skirt and takes off her garter, the men stare at her pretty leg. Iago whistles lewdly, and she flounces her skirt down. Bending, he uses the garter as a tourniquet.)* So! O, for a chair to bear him easily hence. *(Cassio's head falls suddenly.)*

Bianca: Alas, he faints! O Cassio, Cassio, Cassio!

Iago: Gentlemen all, I do suspect this trash...*(He points at Bianca.)*...to be a party in this injury. *(To the unconscious officer)* Patience awhile, good Cassio. *(To the others, as he starts to explore further.)* Lend me a light. *(His search ends at the body of Roderigo, where he holds the torch close to the face of the corpse.)* Know we this face or no? *(A gasp of horror)* Alas, my friend and my dear countryman Roderigo? No...yes, sure! O Heaven! Roderigo!

Gratiano: (Following to look also) What, of Venice?

Iago: (As he kneels by the man he has just killed.) Even he, sir! Did you know him?

Gratiano: Know him? Ay!

Iago: (He returns to the victim still alive.) How do you, Cassio? *(Calling out to the neighborhood.)* O, a chair, a chair!

Gratiano: (With an attempt to revive the corpse.) Roderigo?

Iago: (Agreeing hastily about the identification as he pulls Gratiano away from the dead man.) He, he, tis he! *(Neighbors bring in a chair, and carefully they seat Cassio on it as a make-shift stretcher.)* Some good man bear him carefully from hence. I'll fetch the general's surgeon. *(Pushing away Bianca, who is trying to help.)* For you, mistress, save you your labor. *(To Cassio, who has revived with the movement, he makes inquiry about Roderigo.)* He that lies slain here was my dear friend. What malice was between you?

Cassio: (Looking at the corpse from his chair.) None in the world, nor do I know the man.

Iago: What, look you pale? *(To the townsfolk, who carry Cassio.)* O, bear him out of the air. *(As Cassio is taken off, Iago keeps Gratiano and Lodovico from following.)* Stay you, good gentlemen. *(He accuses Bianca of helping cause the night attack.)* Look you pale, mistress? *(To the gentlemen)* Behold her well. I pray you, look upon her. *(Bianca becomes confused.)* Do you see, gentlemen? Nay, guiltiness will speak!

Emilia: (As she enters in her night-robe, awakened by the noise.) Alas, what's the matter? What's the matter, husband?

Iago: Cassio hath here been set on in the dark by Roderigo and fellows that are 'scaped. He's almost slain, and Roderigo dead!

Emilia: (Gazing at Roderigo's corpse) Alas, good gentleman! Alas, good Cassio!

Iago: (With a religious air) This is the fruit of whoring! Prithee, Emilia, go know of Cassio where he supped tonight. *(As she starts away, he stops her and watches Bianca closely.)* What, do you shake at that?

Bianca: (Trembling) He supped at my house. But I therefore shake not.

Iago: O, did he so? *(As a military officer, he holds her for questioning.)* I charge you, go with me!

Emilia: (In a haughty fashion to the courtesan.) Fie, fie upon thee, strumpet!

Bianca: *(Pretending to be respectable)* I am no strumpet, but of life as honest as you!

Emilia: As I? Foh! Fie upon thee! *(Forgetting her recent jokes on whoring, she looks quite proper.)*

Iago: *(To the men)* Kind gentlemen, let's go see poor Cassio dressed. *(To Bianca, harshly)* Come, mistress, you must tell us another tale! *(To his wife)* Emilia, run you to the Citadel and tell my lord and lady what hath happed. *(Emilia leaves, and Iago motions for the others to go ahead while he kneels to pray over dead Roderigo.)* Will you go on afore?

(All exit. Iago makes the sign of the cross piously over the corpse before taking Roderigo's rings and pocket money. He bites his lip with excitement and suspense, for his plans are all afoot, win or lose.) This is the night that either makes me or for-does me quite! *(He leaves, dragging the dead Roderigo by the foot.)*

Scene 2

(In her chamber, Desdemona lies asleep in the curtained bed, her white lace robe drawn about her. A candle burns nearby. Othello enters and walks slowly to the bed. There he pauses to study her pale beauty by the candlelight, mourning the necessary justice of her death.)

Othello: It is the cause, it is the cause, my soul! *(He looks upward to Heaven.)* Let me not name it to you, you chaste stars. It is the cause! Yet I'll not shed her blood nor scar that whiter skin of hers than snow and smooth as monumental alabaster. Yet she must die, else she'll betray more men.

(Gazing at the candle) Put out the light and... *(Gazing at Desdemona)*...then "put out the light." *(To the candle)* If I quench thee, thou flaming minister, I can again thy former light restore, should I repent me. *(To his sleeping wife, whose flame of life, once dead, will never find divine fire to revive her.)* But once put out **thy** light, thou cunningst pattern of excelling nature, I know not where is that Promethean heat that can thy light re-lume.

(Drawing near to smell the scent of her skin.) When I have plucked the rose, I cannot give it vital growth again. It needs must wither. I'll smell thee on the tree. *(He kisses her softly and turns away in sorrow.)* O balmy breath, that dost almost persuade Justice to break her sword. One more...*(He kisses her again.)*... one more!... *(And again).* Be thus when thou art dead, and I will kill thee and love thee after. One more and this the last! *(Again a light kiss)* So sweet was ne'er so fatal! I must weep, but they are cruel tears. This sorrow's heavenly; it strikes where it doth love. *(Desdemona stirs.)* She wakes.

(Afraid to look into her beloved eyes, he turns his back to put the candle down.)

Desdemona: (Alarmed) Who's there? Othello?

Othello: Ay, Desdemona.

Desdemona: (Timidly) Will you come to bed, my lord?

Othello: (Sternly, still not looking at her.) Have you prayed tonight, Desdemona?

Desdemona: Ay, my lord.

Othello: (From the wall he takes a cross and holds it towards her, for she must quickly pray for any unforgiven sins.) If you bethink yourself of any crime unreconciled as yet to Heaven and grace, solicit for it straight!

Desdemona: (Uneasily) Alack, my lord, what may you mean by that?

(Her question, when she seems so guilty, enrages Othello, and he thrusts the cross into her hands with ruthless haste.)

Othello: Well, do it and be brief! *(She looks at him, pale in the darkness, and he turns away from her beauty.)* I will walk by. I would not kill thy unprepared spirit. *(A cry of desperate love.)* No, Heaven forfend! I would not kill thy soul!

Desdemona: (Stunned) Talk you of killing?

Othello: Ay, I do!

Desdemona: (She kisses the cross he has given her.) Then Heaven have mercy on me!

Othello: Amen, with all my heart!

Desdemona: (Like a trusting child) If you say so, I hope you will not kill me.

Othello: (A barbaric grunt) Hum .... *(Approaching her again, he looks back and forth across the bed where he believes she sinned with Cassio.)*

Desdemona: And yet I fear you, for you're fatal then when your eyes roll so. Why I should fear, I know not, since guiltiness I know not. But yet I feel I fear!

Othello: (Amazed that she tells lies at such a time.) Think on thy sins!

Desdemona: They are loves I bear to you!

Othello: (In mockery) Ay, and for that thou diest! *(He bites his lower lip.)*

Desdemona: That death's unnatural that kills for loving. Alas, why gnaw you so your nether lip? *(He shudders with jealousy.)* Some bloody passion shakes your very frame!

Othello: (Harshly trying to regain his calm) Peace and be still!

Desdemona: I will so. *(There is a pause, and she reaches out her hand to plead with him to explain.)* What's the matter?

Othello: (Giving her a last chance to confess, he accuses her outright for the first time.) That handkerchief which I so loved and gave thee... thou gavest to Cassio!

Desdemona: No, by my life and soul! *(With desperate inspiration)* Send for the man and ask him!

Othello: (Demanding truth, for she must not die with a lie on her lips.) Sweet soul, take heed, take heed of perjury. Thou art on thy deathbed!

Desdemona: Ay, but not yet to die! *(Her voice quivers.)*

Othello: Therefore confess thee freely of thy sin! *(Seizing the cross, he holds it high before her.)* Thou art to die!

Desdemona: (Looking at the cross) Then... Lord have mercy on me...

Othello: (In a thundering roar) I say, "Amen!" *(He dashes the cross to the floor.)*

Desdemona: (Praying for him also)... and have you mercy too! *(Othello advances on her, his great hands outstretched. She shrinks back, speaking rapidly.)* I never did offend you in my life, never loved Cassio. I never gave him token!

Othello: (Savagely) By Heaven, I saw my handkerchief in his hand! I saw the handkerchief!

Desdemona: (Crouching to the back of the curtained bed, fearfully.) He found it then! I never gave it him! *(With a last plea)* Send for him hither. Let him confess a truth!

Othello: (The voice of doom) He hath confessed!

Desdemona: What, my lord?

Othello: That he hath... "used" thee!

Desdemona: (Refusing to believe it) He will not say so!

Othello: (With a bleak smile of revenge.) No, his mouth is stopped. Honest Iago hath taken order for it!

Desdemona: (Coming forward on the bed.) O, my fear interprets!... What, is he dead? *(Othello nods.)* Alas, he is betrayed and I undone!

Desdemona: Kill me tomorrow. Let me live tonight!

(She begins to cry hopelessly, knowing no one will believe her innocence. Othello takes the tears to be for her dead lover, and they enrage him to murderous action.)

Othello: Out, strumpet! Weepst thou for him to my face? *(He grasps her by the hair.)*

Desdemona: (In a panic) O, banish me, my lord, but kill me not!

Othello: (Forcing her backwards upon the bed, he takes the small pillow with his free hand.) Down, strumpet!

Desdemona: Kill me tomorrow. Let me live tonight!

(She tries to break free, but he kneels on the bed, straddling her slender body, and grips the pillow with both hands. She begins to fight for her life.)

Othello: Nay, if you strive....

Desdemona: ...but half an hour!...

Othello: Being done, there is no pause!

Desdemona: ...but while I say one prayer!...

Othello: (In a great voice) It is too late!

(With primitive passion, he holds the pillow over her face to smother her. Her limbs thrash and then grow still. For a long pause he keeps the pillow harshly pushed upon her while he pants with wild release. There is a knock at the door, then a series of knocks like an alarm. From outside Emilia calls loudly.)

Emilia: My lord, my lord! What ho, my lord, my lord!

Othello: What noise is this? *(He removes the pillow. Desdemona lies still, her neck at an odd angle.)* Not dead? Not yet quite dead? *(He will give her an easy death.)* I that am cruel am yet merciful. I would not have thee linger in thy pain. *(He presses the pillow over her face again, growing calmer.)* So... so....

Emilia: (Outside) What, ho! My lord, my lord!

Othello: (To himself) Yes, tis Emilia. *(He shouts out to her.)* By and by! *(He removes the pillow again and looks at his wife.)* She's dead!

(As Emilia continues to knock, he speaks to himself.) Tis like she comes to speak of Cassio's death. The noise was high. *(Again inspecting Desdemona, he moves her head, which loosely turns back and forth.)* Ha! No more moving? Still as the grave.*(Emilia knocks again.)* Shall she come in? Were it good? *(Desdemona's hand slips from the bed and hangs limply.)* I think she stirs again. *(He feels her pulse.)* No.

(Emilia's noise disturbs him and will bring others.) What's best to do? If she come in, she'll sure speak to my wife. My wife? My wife! *(He looks at the lovely form of his bride, pale and still.)* What wife? *(A long, deep shuddering breath.)* I have no wife!

O heavy hour! *(In astonishment he slowly stares about the room, wondering why Nature is not upset also with eclipse and earthquake.)* Methinks it should be now a huge eclipse of sun and moon, and that the affrighted globe should yawn at alteration.

Emilia: (Pleading loudly) I do beseech you that I may speak with you, O good my lord!

Othello: (Absent-mindedly) I had forgot thee. *(He starts towards the door in a daze.)* O, come in, Emilia. *(Turning back)* Soft, by and by... let me the curtains draw. *(As he pulls the bed curtains together to half-hide Desdemona's body, he speaks to her departed soul.)* Where art thou? *(Shaking his head, he crosses to un-bolt the door. Emilia rushes in.)* What's the matter with thee now?

Emilia: O my good lord... *(She points behind her to the street.)*... yonder's foul murders done!

Othello: What? Now?

Emilia: But now, my lord!

Othello: (Half to himself, blaming the moon for such lunatic actions.) It is the very error of the moon. She comes more near the earth than she was wont and makes men mad!

Emilia: Cassio, my lord, hath killed a young Venetian called Roderigo!

Othello: (Slowly) Roderigo killed? And Cassio killed?

Emilia: No, Cassio is not killed.

Othello: (Thunderstruck) Not Cassio killed?

Desdemona: (In a faint voice, not moving.) O, falsely, falsely murdered!

Emilia: (In deep fear) Out and alas! That was my lady's voice. *(She pushes Othello away and runs to the bed. When she sweeps aside the curtains, she stares and cries out loudly.)* Help! Help, ho! Help! *(To her dear young mistress.)* O lady, speak again! Sweet Desdemona! O sweet mistress, speak!

Desdemona: (Weakly) A guiltless death I die.

Emilia: (In a fury for revenge.) O, who hath done this deed?

Desdemona: (With love still in her dying voice.) Nobody . . . I myself. Farewell! *(She gasps.)* Commend me to my kind lord. *(A cry)* O, farewell! *(She dies.)*

Othello: (Pretending ignorance) Why, how should she be murdered?

Emilia: (Suspicious and wary) Alas, who knows? *(She backs away and starts edging towards the door, her eyes on Othello.)*

Othello: You heard her say "herself." It was not I.

Emilia: (Fiercely honest) She said so. I must needs report the truth.

Othello: (Cruelly) She's like a liar gone to burning Hell! *(In a loud voice, confessing.)* 'Twas I that killed her!

Emilia: (In horror) O, the more angel she, and you the blacker devil!

Othello: She was a whore!

Emilia: Thou art a devil! *(Her anger is equal to his.)*

Othello: She was false as water.

Emilia: O, she was heavenly true!

Othello: (Harshly) Cassio did "top" her! Ask thy husband else. Thy husband knew it all.

Emilia: That she was false to wedlock?

Othello: Ay, with Cassio! *(If she had been faithful, he would value her above a world made of a single golden gem.)* Nay, had she been true, if Heaven would make me such another world of one entire and perfect chrysolite, I'd not have sold her for it! *(He breaks into sobs.)*

Emilia: (Rushing to her dead beloved mistress in a burst of grief.) O mistress, villainy hath made mocks with love! *(She throws herself by Desdemona and turns savagely to look on Othello.)* My husband say that she was false?

Othello: He, woman. I say, thy husband! *(His voice cracks.)* Dost understand the word? My friend, thy husband—honest, honest Iago!

Emilia: If he say so, may his soul rot half a grain a day. He lies to the heart! *(Othello is startled. Darting by him, she goes to the door and cries an alarm.)* Help! Help! Ho! Help! The Moor hath killed my mistress! Murder! Murder! *(At her cries, the former governor Montano, Old Gratiano, Iago and others enter.)*

Montano: What is the matter?

Emilia: (To Iago, while she points at the Moor.) He says thou toldst him that his wife was false! *(With hope)* I know thou didst not.

Iago: I told him what I thought and told no more than what he found himself was true.

Emilia: But did you ever tell him she was false?

Iago: I did!

Emilia: You told a lie, a wicked lie! *(Shouting)* She false with Cassio? Did you say with Cassio?

Iago: With Cassio, mistress. *(He bids her be still.)* Go to, charm your tongue!

Emilia: *(Vigorously)* I will not "charm my tongue." I am bound to speak! *(To all the men, as she points, she tells the truth.)* My mistress here lies murdered in her bed!

Othello: Nay, stare not, masters. It is true indeed.

Gratiano: Tis a strange truth! *(They rush towards the bed but stop short at the sight of the dead lady.)*

Emilia: *(In hysterics)* Villainy, villainy, villainy!

Iago: *(Trying to shake her out of her fit.)* What, are you mad? I charge you, get you home.

Emilia: *(She stops her cries suddenly and backs away from him.)* Good gentlemen, let me have leave to speak! *(She eludes her husband's grasp.)* Tis proper I obey him, but not now. *(In defiance)* Perchance, Iago, I will ne'er go home!

Othello: *(In a passion for his loss, he sinks on the bed.)* O! O! O!

Emilia: *(With scorn)* Nay, lay thee down and roar, for thou hast killed the sweetest innocent that e'er did lift up eye!

Othello: O, she was foul! *(Rising, he belatedly recognizes Old Gratiano, Desdemona's uncle.)* I scarce did know you, uncle.

Gratiano: (Advancing to kneel by his niece's deathbed.) Poor Desdemona! I am glad thy father's dead. *(He weeps, for Brabantio has died from the shock of her sudden marriage.)* Thy match was mortal to him.

Othello: Tis pitiful! *(Quietly, he calls his faithful friend as witness.)* But yet Iago knows that she with Cassio hath the "act of shame" a thousand times committed. Cassio confessed it. And she did gratify his amorous works with that pledge of love which I first gave her. I saw it in his hand! *(He shudders at the memory.)* It was a handkerchief my father gave my mother!

Emilia: (As understanding suddenly breaks) O Heaven! O heavenly powers! *(She looks at Iago, realizing his whole plot.)*

Iago: (Out of the side of his mouth, a venomous hiss.) Come, hold your peace!

Emilia: I will not! *(She backs away from him, putting out her hands to protect herself. He draws his sword and follows her.)*

Gratiano: Fie! Your sword upon a woman?

Emilia: (Hurriedly telling the truth.) O thou dull Moor, that handkerchief thou speakst of—I found by fortune and did give my husband, for often he begged of me to steal it!

Iago: (With a lunge of his sword.) Villainous whore! *(She dodges in time.)*

Emilia: She give it Cassio? *(She runs to shout into Othello's face.)* No, alas, I found it! And I did give it my husband! *(Othello stands aghast.)*

Iago: Filth, thou liest!

Othello: (He sees the truth, and, with barbaric fury, he draws his sword to lunge at Iago.) Precious villain! *(Montano steps between the two and disarms Othello. In the confusion, Iago runs his blade through Emilia viciously and, with a laugh of defiance, makes his escape.)*

Gratiano: The woman falls! Sure, he hath killed his wife!

Emilia: (Knowing her wound is mortal.) Aye, aye. *(Her last request takes all her strength.)* O, lay me by my mistress' side....

Gratiano: He's gone, but his wife's killed!

Montano: Tis a notorious villain! *(To Gratiano)* Take you this weapon which I have here recovered from the Moor. *(The two men, carrying Othello's sword, back towards the door, watching the great African carefully for signs of attack.)* Come, guard the door without. Let him not pass but kill him rather. *(Montano intends to pursue Iago.)* I'll after that same villain, for tis a damned slave! *(All leave but Othello and the wounded Emilia.)*

Othello: (In a daze) I am not valiant neither. But why should honor outlive honesty? Let it go all....

(Gently he turns to the dying Emilia, picks her up, and lays the faithful companion at the feet of the faithful wife.)

Emilia: (In a fading voice to the dead Desdemona.) What did thy song bode, lady? Hark, canst thou hear me? I will play the swan and die in music. *(Softly she sings a phrase of Desdemona's song.)* "Willow, willow, willow . . . ."

(Othello kneels by the bed, sobbing quietly. Emilia puts her hand on his.) Moor, she was chaste. She loved thee, cruel Moor! *(Heaven will be Emilia's reward for telling the truth.)* So come my soul to bliss, as I speak true. So speaking as I think, I die . . . I die. *(She closes her eyes in death.)*

Othello: (He kneels for a moment but arouses himself with a quick impulse.) I have another weapon in this chamber. It is a sword of Spain, the ice-brook's temper. *(He finds it behind a chest of clothes.)* O, here it is. *(At the door, sword in hand, he calls through the panels.)* Uncle, I must come forth!

Gratiano: (Coming in slowly with fear on his old face.) What is the matter? *(He raises his sword hurriedly when he sees Othello armed, but the Moor does not try to fight.)*

Othello: Behold, I have a weapon. I have seen the day that, with this little arm and this good sword, I have made my way through more impediments than twenty times your stop. But O, vain boast! *(To the unlucky stars)* Who can control his fate? *(To Old Gratiano with a faint smile.)* Be not afraid, though you do see me weaponed. Here is my journey's end.

(Turning, he walks to his dead love.) Now, how dost thou look now? O ill-starred wench . . . pale as thy smock. *(She will meet him in Heaven before he goes to Hell.)* When we shall meet, this look of thine will hurl my soul from Heaven, and fiends will snatch at it! *(He takes her innocent hand.)* Cold, cold, my girl? Even like thy chastity.

(With rage at Iago, his false servant.) O cursed, cursed slave! *(He kneels beside his beloved bride and buries his face in her hair.)* O Desdemona! Desdemona. Dead! O! O! O!

(Lodovico, Montano and officers enter with Iago taken prisoner, his arms tied behind him. Old Gratiano greets them with relief. Cassio follows, carried in a chair, his leg heavily bandaged. At first Lodovico does not see Othello, who is half-hidden by the bed curtains.)

Lodovico: Where is this rash and most unfortunate man?

Othello: (Speaking of himself as if already dead.) That's he that was Othello? Here I am. *(He rises to face them.)*

Lodovico: (With a gesture to Iago's guards.) Where is that viper? Bring the villain forth.

Othello: (Staring down to see if Iago has the cloven hoofs of the Devil.) I look down towards his feet . . . but that's a fable. *(To Iago)* If that thou be'st a devil, I cannot kill thee! *(Taking his icy steel sword, he lunges at him.)*

Lodovico: Wrench his sword from him! *(The guards disarm the Moor.)*

Iago: (On a note of victory.) I bleed, sir, but not killed!

Othello: I am not sorry neither. *(A death wish)* I'd have thee live, for in my sense, tis happiness to die.

Lodovico: (With great pity) O thou Othello, that wert once so good, what shall be said to thee?

Othello: Why, anything. *(In explanation he speaks with a warrior's simple code.)* An honorable murderer, if you will, for naught I did in hate but all in honor.

Lodovico: (Pointing to Iago) This wretch hath part confessed his villainy. Did you and he consent in Cassio's death?

Othello: (Sadly) Ay.

Cassio: Dear general, I never gave you cause! *(He looks at the Moor with deep devotion.)*

Othello: (Clasping Cassio's hand) I do believe it, and I ask your pardon. *(Cassio turns his head aside to weep, as Othello pleads to find the reason for Iago's treachery.)* Will you, I pray, demand that demi-devil why he hath thus ensnared my soul and body?

Iago: (Defiantly) Demand me—nothing! What you know, you know. From this time forth I never will speak word!

Lodovico: What, not to pray?

Gratiano: (With the threat of the torture chamber.) Torments will ope your lips! *(But Iago clamps his lips tightly together and shakes his head. He will not give the gentlemen the satisfaction of an explanation.)*

Othello: Well, thou dost best. *(He sighs and sits heavily, a broken man.)*

Cassio: Most heathenish and most gross!

Othello: (To Cassio, quietly) How came you, Cassio, by that handkerchief that was my wife's?

Cassio: I found it in my chamber. *(Looking at Iago, who smiles in silence.)* And he himself confessed that there he dropped it.

Othello: (Beating his own chest with his fist.) O fool! Fool! Fool!

Lodovico: (With ceremony, he puts Othello under arrest.) You must forsake this room and go with us. Your power and your command is taken off, and Cassio rules in Cyprus. *(Othello bows his head and removes his gold chain-of-office, which he puts about Cassio's neck. For a moment they embrace. But Othello moves away, leaving Cassio to weep.)*

(The guards come to take Othello's arms and lead him off, but he stops them with a gesture of command.)

Othello: Soft you, a word or two before you go!

(The guards pause while he goes to Desdemona's deathbed. All watch with understanding. Othello takes Desdemona's hand and kisses it in farewell. Then he turns, suddenly erect, like the great calm general that they knew before the tragedy. His voice rings out.)

I have done the State some service, and they know it. *(But he shrugs off his heroic past.)* No more of that! I pray you, in your letters, speak of me as I am. *(With absolute justice, he wants no excuses, no hatred.)* Nothing extenuate, nor set down aught in malice. Then must you speak of one that loved . . . not wisely, but too well! Of one not easily jealous but, being wrought, perplexed in the extreme. *(He looks at his dead love.)* Of one whose hand, like the base Indian, threw a pearl away richer than all his tribe. Set you down this!

(As his friends nod agreement, Othello puts his hand into his robe to grip a hidden dagger. He begins a story of a foreigner who attacked a Venetian and cursed the city in Othello's presence.) And say, besides, that in Aleppo once, where a malignant and a turbaned Turk beat a Venetian and traduced the State . . . I took by the throat the circumcised dog and smote him . . . thus! *(He raises his dagger high and stabs himself in the chest.)*

Lodovico: O bloody period!

Othello: (To his dead bride with tender love.) I kissed thee ere I killed thee. No way but this . . . killing myself, to die upon a kiss! *(With a last touch of his wife's pale lips, he falls across her body and dies.)*

Cassio: This did I fear, but thought he had no weapon. For he was great of heart!

Lodovico: (To Iago, still silent) O Spartan dog, look on the tragic loading of this bed. This is thy work. *(To the others)* Let it be hid. *(Slowly they draw the curtains to hide the bodies of Othello, Desdemona and Emilia.)*

(To Old Gratiano, he gives the Moor's estate.) Gratiano, keep the house and fortunes of the Moor, for they succeed on you. *(To Cassio he turns over the task of sentencing Iago.)* To you, Lord Governor, remains the censure of this hellish villain—the time, the place, the torture. O, enforce it! *(Cassio bows, gravely accepting his high position.)*

(Lodovico himself will return to Venice with the sad story.) Myself will straight aboard and to the State this heavy act with heavy heart relate. *(Sadly and slowly, they leave the chamber of death.)*

FINIS

SOME FAMOUS QUOTATIONS

Iago: Mere "prattle without practice" is all his soldiership. *(ACT I, Scene 1)*

Iago: I will wear my heart upon my sleeve. *(ACT I, Scene 1)*

Othello: Most potent, grave and reverend Signiors, my very noble and approved good masters...I will a round, un-varnished tale deliver. *(ACT I, Scene 3)*

Othello: She loved me for the dangers I had passed...and I loved her that she did pity them! *(ACT I, Scene 3)*

Desdemona: O most lame and impotent conclusion! *(ACT II, Scene 1)*

Othello: If it were now to die, 'twere now to be most happy! *(ACT II, Scene 1)*

Iago: But men are men! The best sometimes forget. *(ACT II, Scene 3)*

Cassio: Reputation, reputation, reputation! O, I have lost my reputation! I have lost the immortal part of myself, and what remains is bestial. *(ACT II, Scene 3)*

Cassio: O thou invisible spirit of wine, if thou hast no name to be known by, let us call thee, "Devil"!... O God, that men should put an enemy in their mouths, to steal away their brains! *(ACT II, Scene 3)*

Iago: Come, come, good wine is a good familiar creature, if it be well used. *(ACT II, Scene 3)*

Iago: How poor are they that have not patience! What wound did ever heal but by degrees? *(ACT II, Scene 3)*

Iago: Pleasure and action make the hours seem short! *(ACT II, Scene 3)*

Othello: Excellent wretch! Perdition catch my soul, but I do love thee! And when I love thee not, Chaos is come again. *(ACT III, Scene 3)*

Iago: Who steals my purse, steals trash: tis something... nothing. 'Twas mine, tis his, and has been slave to thousands. But he that filches from me my good name, robs me of that which not enriches him and makes me poor indeed. *(ACT III, Scene 3)*

Iago: O beware, my lord, of jealousy! It is the green-eyed monster. *(ACT III, Scene 3)*

Emilia: But jealous souls will not be answered so. They are not ever "jealous for the cause" but "jealous for they're jealous." *(ACT III, Scene 4)*

Othello: But yet the pity of it, Iago! O Iago, the pity of it, Iago! *(ACT IV, Scene 1)*

Desdemona: I understand a fury in your words, but not the words. *(ACT IV, Scene 2)*

Desdemona: Sing willow, willow, willow. *(ACT IV, Scene 3)*

Iago: He hath a daily beauty in his life. *(ACT V, Scene 1)*

Othello: It is the very error of the moon. She comes more near the earth than she was wont and makes men mad. *(ACT V, Scene 2)*

Othello: If Heaven would make me such another world of one entire and perfect chrysolite, I'd not have sold her for it! *(ACT V, Scene 2)*

Othello: Who can control his fate? *(ACT V, Scene 2)*

Othello: I have done the State some service, and they know it. *(ACT V, Scene 2)*

Othello: Then must you speak of one that loved... not wisely, but too well!... Of one whose hand, like the base Indian, threw a pearl away richer than all his tribe. *(ACT V, Scene 2)*